HARPER AND THE ONE-NIGHT STAND

Novel #3

R. LINDA

HARPER AND THE ONE-NIGHT STAND

Copyright © 2018 by R. Linda.
All rights reserved.
First Print Edition: March 2018

Limitless Publishing, LLC
Kailua, HI 96734
www.limitlesspublishing.com

Formatting: Limitless Publishing

ISBN-13: 978-1-64034-350-4
ISBN-10: 1-64034-350-4

DEDICATION

To my mum.
Thank you for…everything.
Love you x

PROLOGUE

THEN

Harper

The thing about one-night stands was they were supposed to be just that.

One night.

One night of fun. One night of no strings. No commitment.

But sometimes a one-night stand wouldn't go away. It kept reoccurring, against your better judgement. Sometimes a one-night stand was exactly what you needed—over and over again. But then it wasn't really a one-night stand anymore. It became something else entirely, even when you didn't want it to. It became something you couldn't walk away from, even though you knew you should. Even though you knew it couldn't continue without hurting someone else.

But sometimes…

You. Just. Couldn't. Walk. Away.

Sometimes you found yourself waking up in their bed when you should have been home alone in your own.

Sometimes you found yourself doing the walk of shame at the crack of dawn, attempting to sneak past their roommate's door before anyone found out you were in the one place you both knew you shouldn't have been.

With my heels in my hands, I crept down the hallway that had become as familiar to me as my own, silently trying to escape before anyone woke up. The sun had barely risen, so I knew it was early. I should have felt guilty for sneaking out, but I knew even though it might hurt him to find his bed empty again, he'd understand. He didn't want this getting out of hand any more than I did. He didn't want anyone finding out about our...extracurricular activities either.

We knew we were asking for trouble. We knew if we didn't stop this, it would blow up in our faces. Yet we continued. There was something that kept bringing us back together. No matter how hard I tried to resist, all it took was one smile, and I was putty in his hands. But it was getting risky, and we really needed to stop.

"Don't forget your purse," Linc called from the kitchen. I froze, one foot on the fluffy grey rug, the other on the cold timber floorboards. Four more steps and I would have been free. Linc walked into the living room where I was contemplating running, and he had my purse in his hands. "Wouldn't want anyone know you were here again last night, would we?"

Again?

I turned to face him, my fingers fiddling with the straps on my heels. "How long?"

"How long, what?" He raised a questioning eyebrow and threw my purse down on the coffee table beside me.

"How long have you known?"

He laughed and clapped his hands on his legs. "That it was you? About a month. That he'd been sneaking someone in here every couple of weeks? Since we got back from Fiji." He turned away from me and walked back into the kitchen. "Coffee?" he called over his shoulder.

My eyes widened, and I rushed after him into the small room, stopping on the other side of the counter. "Fiji was three months ago."

"Walls are thin, sunshine." He handed me a cup of black coffee and placed the smallest scoop of sugar into his.

My cheeks warmed in embarrassment. Oh, god, he'd heard. I took a gulp of the liquid gold in my hands, scalding my throat, but I barely noticed. He'd heard.

"Don't worry. I have noise cancelling headphones."

"You can't say anything," I pleaded, clutching the coffee cup to my chest. "To anyone."

"You're playing with fire, you know." He narrowed his gaze on me, bringing his mug to his lips and taking a long, slow sip.

"I know." I hoisted myself on the barstool at the counter and ran my hands through my hair. "But please don't say anything. I don't want anyone to

3

get hurt."

It was only supposed to be one night. One night of too many drinks and one morning in Fiji, waking up to find myself in his bed with no memory of the night before.

He lifted a shoulder casually and leaned against the counter, facing me. "I'll be quiet."

"You will?" I sagged in relief.

"He's my mate. And I know exactly what it feels like to want the one person you know you shouldn't want, remember?" His smile was full of understanding, and in that moment, I knew Linc would keep our secret. At least for now. He'd secretly been in love with his best mate's younger sister almost their entire lives, so he understood the struggle and the need for silence.

"But I don't…It's not like—"

"I don't care what it's like. It's none of my business. But you both need to figure this shit out now, before either of you gets too attached and anyone else becomes collateral damage. If this is only something casual, end it now before you hurt either of them."

"I don't want to hurt them."

"Then you need to figure it out."

"Do you really think it'll hurt Brody?" Even asking the question, I knew I sounded like an insensitive ass. Of course, it would hurt him. And that was the last thing I wanted. But there was something about Nate Kellerman that had me coming back for more.

"His cousin sleeping with his ex-girlfriend?" He screwed his face up and nodded. "Yeah, it'll sting.

4

Just a little."

Just a little.

It wouldn't hurt just a little. It would hurt a lot.

I needed to end this now. I didn't want to be the cause of anyone's pain.

"I'll end it." I sighed and lowered my head to the counter. I didn't want to hurt Brody or lead Nate on if I didn't know where this was going. Because, really, I didn't know what I wanted. I didn't want a relationship, but I liked the way Nate made me feel. "It's done. As soon as he wakes up, I'll tell him no more."

Linc didn't speak. He just eyed me sceptically and nodded once before pouring his coffee down the sink. "Good."

He picked up his surfboard that was leaning against the wall in the corner and left. He left me sitting there alone, waiting for Nate to wake up so I could end what it was between us before things got any more out of control.

Chapter One

Nate

The smell of grease permeated the air, so thick I nearly choked on it. I liked fried meat as much as the next guy, but this was almost unbearable. The woman scrubbing the counter smiled as I walked in. How this place had the best burgers in the state, I didn't know, but Ryder raved about it, so there I was, waiting for my sister to arrive. She and her friends had finally finished university and were coming home. For how long, I wasn't sure, but she'd been gone three years, and the last six months had been the most painful. Not because I missed her or anything like that, which I did, but because I had to deal with my lovesick best mate and his obsession with my sister.

It was weird.

As much as I was okay with their relationship— they were made for each other—it was still weird. I couldn't wrap my head around the fact the guy I had been friends with for twenty-three years was dating my younger sister.

Weird.

I located an empty booth in the back corner of the fifties-inspired diner at the roadhouse on the outskirts of town. Again, how Ryder even knew this place was here was beyond me. I had never stopped here for anything other than to put fuel in the car when it was running on fumes and had no clue there was even a place to eat. But there I sat, watching the killer storm brewing outside while I waited for everyone to arrive.

I was browsing the unappealing menu when the doors finally opened and in walked Indie and Linc, a whirl of air rushing around them. That storm was going to hit sooner rather than later. I was out of my seat and scooping my sister into my arms the moment the doors closed behind them.

Indie laughed. "Good to see you too, big bro."

"Sorry, it's just good to have you home. I won't have to deal with listening to this one," I gestured at Lincoln, "bitch and moan about when he could see you next any longer." I released her and led them over to the booth I had claimed in the deserted diner.

"Aww, did you miss me, stupid ass?" Indie teased Linc, using a nickname I didn't understand and wasn't sure I wanted to.

"Ace," he said through clenched teeth. Another nickname I didn't want to know how it originated. The less I knew about my sister's relationship with my best friend, the better.

Weird.

"How was the drive?" I asked, sliding into the

booth opposite them.

Indie coughed and shot Linc a strange look while he lounged back against the seat with a smug look on his face. "Good, man. It was…real…good."

Indie smiled and slapped him on the chest, and I groaned. I didn't want any more details. She pulled out her phone and frowned.

"Where's Bailey? She and Ryder passed us hours ago. She should have let me know by now they had made it home safely."

"I'm sure they're fine," Linc reassured her.

"They passed you? How?" I knew they were back. In fact, I had seen them both an hour ago. But Indie didn't know that, and she didn't need to.

"Umm…" Indie hesitated and looked at Linc for an answer. She obviously didn't get the one she was hoping for, because she continued with a note of hesitancy in her voice. "We stopped…for…umm, fuel…and food. Yes, food. Can't have a road trip without an appropriate amount of snacks to keep your energy up." Her smile was too bright. Her eyes too wide. She was lying. They didn't stop for fuel and snacks. But I really didn't want to know why they stopped.

"Well, maybe Bailey and Ryder stopped for snacks too somewhere along the way," I suggested.

Indie giggled into her hand like a teenage boy hearing the word "boobs" and muttered, "Yeah, I bet they did. Bailey likes snacks…"

"She needs them. For energy." Linc coughed into his shoulder.

"Stamina." Indie bit her fist.

"And Ryder is always fully fuelled and ready to

go." Linc lost it. He threw his head back and laughed.

Indie bit her lip to stop herself from laughing but failed, and pretty soon they had tears streaming down their faces.

I was missing something. They were definitely talking about something other than snacks and fuel. I knew exactly what it sounded like, but I wasn't quite ready to admit to myself what that might be, so I pushed the thought aside and tried to not think about it.

Thankfully, a moment later, the perfect distraction arrived. All thoughts of fuel, snacks, and stamina were forgotten the moment the kitchen doors opened and out walked Harper. She had her head down and wasn't looking in our direction, but I knew it was her. I'd know her shoulder length black hair and the way it brushed the top of her neck anywhere. I'd spent a lot of time with my hands in her hair and lips on her neck. What was she doing here?

I lifted my hand to wave but then thought better of it and ran my hand through my hair instead. Great cover. She was supposed to be with Kenzie.

"It's just us, then?" Indie asked, stealing my attention from Harper.

"Yep," Linc answered.

Indie frowned.

"You were expecting a welcome home party, In?" I teased. The front doors opened, the wind howled, and the doors slammed shut again. I looked up, and Harper was gone.

"What? No, I just thought our friends and family

would at least like to be here when we got back."
She picked at a napkin on the table.

"What am I? A neighbour?"

"No, I mean…I'm glad you're here, but I
thought Mum and Dad or Kenzie would want to see
us too."

"I'm sure you'll see more than enough of
everybody soon, Ace." Linc kissed the side of her
head before changing the subject. "I'm starving."

He looked over his shoulder and signalled to the
woman behind the counter that we'd like to order.
Not that I really wanted to order anything on the
menu, but we needed to stall a while longer until I
got the text from Ryder saying everything was
ready.

The woman, whose name tag read Julie, came
and took our orders.

Indie yawned. "Man, I'm exhausted. Let's just
eat, and then you can take me to my parents'
house."

"Two minutes ago, you were complaining no one
was throwing you a welcome back party, and now
you want to go to bed?" I fished my phone out of
my pocket when I heard the message tone.

"Shut up. I'm tired. I can change my mind. You
can throw me a party tomorrow instead."

I read the message.

Ryder: Ready when you are.

I looked at Linc and waved my phone so he
knew it was time.

"What was that about?" Indie's eyes flickered

between Linc and me.

"What?" I brushed her question aside and typed a response to Ryder.

Nate: 30 minutes.

"You shook your phone at Linc," she said to me then turned to him. "And you nodded in agreement. You guys just had a secret conversation. Something you don't want me to know about."

"Ace, you're tired. I think you're imagining things. I was just nodding to the music on the jukebox. Elvis rocks," Linc countered with such a definitive edge to his voice that Indie believed him immediately. Had I said that to her, she would have seen right through the lie.

"Maybe you're right."

Julie, the waitress, returned a few minutes later with burgers and Cokes for all of us.

"Oh, I'm starving." Indie thanked her, clapping her hands in excitement.

"Work up a big appetite, Ace?" Linc nudged her with his elbow, but she was already devouring the burger.

"Uh-hmmm…" Her eyes widened, and she chewed, but clearly not fast enough. "This burger is freaking amazing," she mumbled with a mouthful of food, pieces of lettuce falling out of her mouth, and ketchup on her chin.

Linc smiled at her while I screwed up my face in disgust. "Been eating long?"

She didn't even bother with a response, instead choosing to stick her finger up at me while still

11

shoving the burger in her mouth. It must have been good.

I reached for mine, and my eyes just about rolled into the back of my head. Indie and Ryder were right. Best. Burger. Ever.

We ate in silence, savouring every mouthful, and when we finished, I paid the bill. Indie was tired and wanted to leave, but Linc had a surprise for her.

"Ready to go?" I asked, shoving my wallet back into the pocket of my jeans.

"Yes. Are you ready to tell me what's going on?" Indie stood from the booth and stretched.

I risked a glance at Linc, but he had his eyes screwed, deep in thought. He was trying get around this without telling her the truth and ruining everything. Indie had no clue that for the last three months, he'd been spending every day and night fixing up a run-down old shack on the beach, turning it into a cottage they could call home once Indie graduated.

"Nothing is going on, Ace. Your brother's weird. You know that," Linc answered smoothly, grabbing her hand and leading her to the door. "Let's just go. I need to stop somewhere quickly on the way home, but it'll only take a minute."

"Where?" she asked, wrapping one arm around her waist to protect from the chill of the night air when we opened the door and a gust of wind whipped around us.

"Ahh, just a mate's from work. Two seconds, that's all it will take."

Indie groaned in defeat before turning to me and wrapping her arms around me.

"Good to have you home, In. I'll see you tomorrow, yeah?"

She nodded. "Yeah. Bye."

I rushed over to my car, hoping Linc was smart enough to stall so I could get to "The Love Shack," as he named it—even had the plaque on the wall beside the front door—before them. I didn't want to miss Indie's face when she realised it was her home now.

Chapter Two

Harper

I should have gone over and said hello to Nate and welcomed Indie home, but I was too stunned to see them there. In our diner, of all places. Instead, I ducked my head and pretended not to notice them. It would have been too awkward. I had been avoiding Nate Kellerman for three months. He walked into a room, I walked out. But tonight I was going to be crammed into a small cottage with no escape.

I pulled my car to the side of the road just around the corner from "The Love Shack." I laughed at the name, thinking it was genius. But I couldn't have imagined Nate would be too impressed about his sister moving into a house that sounded like a place where sex parties happened. I got out of the car, slammed the door, and jogged up the dirt track—because it wasn't really a road, it was gravel, and not much of it—toward the shack. Indie wouldn't have recognised my car, but I thought it was best to hide it with everyone else's so it didn't ruin Linc's surprise.

I opened the gate of the little picket fence the guys spent last weekend building and let myself in the back door. The only access to the house was through the back. The front had a wraparound porch that led straight onto the beach—perfect for Linc, since he was basically a fish.

"Surprise!" everyone called as I walked into the kitchen, followed by a chorus of groans.

"Sorry. Sorry." I held my hands up in apology as I approached Nate and Indie's mother. "Need help with anything?"

She had been helping Kenzie and Nate set up all day while I worked, and the woman looked flustered and tired. Her husband was in the living room with Ryder and Brody, having a beer.

"I'm okay, dear. You just go in there and relax." She smiled at me.

I glanced into the small living room and was relieved to see Bailey and Kenzie on the sofa, while Ryder was standing over by the huge window that overlooked the beach with Nate and Indie's dad, and Brody.

"Grab a glass and sit down." Kenzie waved the bottle of wine she and Bailey were sharing in my direction.

Brody looked up at the sound of Kenzie's voice and smiled and gave me a small wave. He must have excused himself from whatever conversation he was having because he was suddenly walking in my direction.

"Harper! Hey, how's it going?" The grin on his

face was too keen. Too eager. He still held a flame that I didn't. We'd dated a few years ago when I was just starting out in university, but it didn't stick. We just weren't right. As awesome as he was, we didn't mesh well together. Besides, I had too much going on with my family to make any relationship work. I had the feeling, though, that he still held on to some residual feelings that weren't going to go away until he moved on. Kind of ironic, since he was the one who left me because I couldn't commit.

But whatever.

"Hey. Good. You?" Small talk was so damn awkward, I didn't know where to begin.

"Can't complain. Though I wish I lived somewhere else sometimes." He chuckled into his fist.

"Oh, really? Why?" This had me interested. Brody was the most easy-going, carefree roommate a person could want. And living with Nate should have been a breeze. The fact he couldn't handle me or my issues was a huge testament to his self-control. I knew he tried to make it work as much as I did, but it simply didn't. I couldn't deal with relationship issues on top of my family issues.

"Nate." He shrugged.

"Nate?" My voice was coarse, hesitant. I didn't know how to react. Calm. Cool. Collected. Or pissed off. Why the hell was Nate making things difficult?

Why was Nate, of all people, making my ex-boyfriend wish he lived somewhere else?

"Yeah…Nate. The girls, the late nights. You know how it goes," he said. "The life of a single man." He laughed.

"Girls?" was all I managed to choke out, my breath getting caught in my throat.

Girls. Single. Available. As in…every other girl but me.

I was single. Available. Ready to mingle, with and without the one person I wanted to mingle with. It was wrong. I knew it. Nate knew it. But there was nothing I could do about it.

"Heartbreak, he reckons. Personally, I just think he likes getting laid."

I couldn't argue there. Not after Fiji and Nate's parents' wedding. One night was all it took to hook me. To have me thinking, dreaming, imagining his smooth, lean, tanned body moving against mine. One night made me so crazy with desire that I couldn't stop myself. I knew it was wrong. Nate was Brody's cousin. Brody, my ex-boyfriend. Our fling broke all the rules, and for the first three months, it was unstoppable, until Linc told me to walk away. It wasn't worth hurting Brody over, and he was right. Brody still didn't know, and for that, I was grateful, because I doubted he'd be standing here talking to me otherwise.

But it still stung to hear Nate had been having the time of his life while I was stagnant. Going through the motions but not really living. I'd lost my spark and zest for life years ago. A poor excuse for a family had that effect on a person. Brody brought me back to life for a little while, but I was too lost, and I knew I'd only drag Brody down with me, so I distanced myself from him, and when it got too much, when family detonated around me, I ran.

17

Brody broke up with me, and we never saw or spoke to each other again until the Kellermans renewed their vows six months ago.

Not knowing what else to say, I smiled and said, "Well, it's good to see you." We hadn't really seen a lot of each other since he moved back to town, with both of us always working and me trying to finish my nursing degree.

Brody's face lit up. "You too."

"Harper!" Kenzie called again, saving me from any more awkwardness with Brody. If we had to make much more small talk, I was sure I'd blurt out that I had been sleeping with his cousin.

"I better go over there." I nodded in the direction of the still waving wine bottle.

"Ah, sure. Right." Brody turned and walked back to Ryder, leaving me standing there stupidly for a moment before Bailey shuffled over and made room for me on the sofa.

"Is it weird?" Bailey asked.

"Is what weird?" I watched Kenzie pour a generous amount of wine into a glass that seemed to appear out of nowhere.

"Having Brody back in town. He's going to always be around now."

I looked over at Brody, who had just answered a phone call. Yes, it was weird, but not for the reasons she expected, obviously.

"No, not all. We can be friends. We dated. We broke up. It was a long time ago." I reached for the glass in Kenzie's hand and gulped half of it down. She quirked one eyebrow at me and smirked, while Bailey scrutinised my face, assessing my reaction. I didn't have a poker face; I gave away everything with one look.

"You're hiding something." Kenzie pointed with the hand holding her wineglass.

"Nope." I looked away, searching for anything that could be a distraction, a way to change the subject and to avoid Kenzie's third degree. It wasn't that I was hiding things from her. I was hiding things from Brody, and I couldn't risk him finding out. They were all so close, and I was still very much the outsider. Someone was bound to open their mouth and tell him.

"Guys, sorry, I gotta go. They're short at work, and I need to cover the shift," Brody said, pocketing his phone and grabbing his jacket. "I'll see Indie tomorrow, I guess." He said goodbye and walked out the door.

I breathed a sigh of relief. With Brody not here, Kenzie would ease up on the inquisition. She was too intuitive for her own good sometimes, always watching and analysing. She saw things most people failed to see, just like her brother, Ryder. There was no hiding anything from them.

"Definitely hiding something. You have shifty eyes."

"You have had too much wine." I pushed her hand away from my face before she stabbed me in the eye with a violet polished fingernail.

"Nathaniel! Really? Sneaking in here quietly like that. I thought it was Indiana." Mrs. K's voice provided the distraction I both needed and didn't want. All our attention turned to the kitchen where Nate was apologising to his mother for sneaking up

19

on her while trying to reach around her to swipe some of the frosting from the "Welcome Home, Indie" cake on the counter.

"They'll be here in two minutes. We left the diner at the same time," Nate announced, giving me a pointed look. He had seen me rush past without stopping. I swallowed more wine, a lump suddenly forming in my throat.

"Oh, good. Get ready, everybody." Mrs. K clapped her hands then threw them in the air. "Nate, quick, I forgot the banner." She darted around the other side of the counter and pulled a tube out of a bag and handed it to Nate. "Hang this right there." She pointed to the exposed timber beam that divided the kitchen from the living room. "So Indie can see it as soon as she walks in."

Nate unrolled the banner, his eyebrows pinched together and his jaw set in a firm line. "No. I'm not hanging that."

"You will do as you're told," his mum scolded, holding out the tape.

"I'm not hanging a banner that says **'Welcome to The Love Shack!'** Why couldn't he just get one that says **'Welcome Home'** like a normal person would?" He shook his head slowly and rolled the banner back up.

"Well, I think it's lovely," his mother argued and waved her hand at the beam again.

"Only because it's Linc." He held the banner out for her to take. "Still not hanging it."

"Fine," Mrs. K huffed and snatched it from him. "Ryder, be a dear and hang this for me."

"Sure." Ryder grinned and elbowed Nate as he

walked past him. "Just here?"

Nate growled and stomped away, muttering something about stupid shacks and his sister.

Ryder hung the banner with an amused expression on his face and stood back, biting his bottom lip. "Looks great. What do you think, Nate?"

Nate took a deep breath. "I think—"

Headlights shone through the kitchen window, silencing Nate and alerting everyone to Indie and Linc's return.

We all stood and gathered under the garishly bright and tacky love shack banner while Nate hung in the background. I glanced over my shoulder—I shouldn't have, but I just couldn't help it—and he was looking right at me. His blue eyes, unblinking, sent shivers down my spine as I took him in. He had this whole James Dean thing going for him now—blue jeans, white t-shirt with the sleeves folded up, short hair slicked back. I liked it. Too much.

"Can't I just wait in the car? It's been a long day. I don't want to—" Indie's voice was muffled from the other side of the back door.

"Two minutes, Ace," Linc said.

The door creaked as he opened it. I turned back around, removing my gaze from Nate's before I did something stupid like kiss him.

"You can't just walk into someone's house, Linc! Oh, my god. I'm waiting outside. This is so embarrassing. I don't know these people, and what if—"

Linc dragged her through the door, cutting off any further argument.

"Surprise!" everyone cheered. Someone whistled. Kenzie, I thought. Someone else threw streamers, and Mrs. K lunged for a stunned Indie.

"Welcome home, precious." She hugged her tight before stepping back and hugging Linc as well.

"I don't understand," Indie said with a wide yet confused smile on her face.

"It's your welcome home party, sweetheart," Indie's dad said, stepping forward to wrap her in his arms then turning to Linc and holding out a hand to shake.

"But?" She looked at each of us in turn before setting her sight on the banner above our heads. "The Love Shack?" She snorted. I pressed my lips together to stop from laughing at her reaction. "Who would name their house The Love Shack?"

"We would, Ace." Linc wrapped an arm around her waist.

"We would?" She turned in his arms and tilted her head back to look at him, her nose scrunched in confusion. "What?"

"Welcome home, princess."

"Welcome home?"

"Are you going to repeat everything I say?"

"Repeat everything you say? Umm…" She looked back at us then up at the banner, a dazed expression on her face.

Linc chuckled and repeated, "Welcome home."

"Home. Our home?" she asked slowly.

Linc leaned in. "Surprise."

Indie looked back at the sign. Her mouth spread into a wide grin. "Oh, my fu—" Mr. K cleared his throat, cutting off Indie's curse. "Fudging god. We have a house!" She jumped on Linc, wrapping her arms around his neck and her legs around his waist, and kissed him. Hard.

It was uncomfortable to see. I fidgeted with the hem of my shirt to avoid watching their open display of affection. Nate stepped in behind me, and the hairs on the back of my neck prickled with awareness.

"All right, get a room, you two," he called before changing his mind. "Actually, no. Don't. No rooms. At all." Linc and Indie pulled apart. Linc had the decency to at least look as though he was sorry for practically mauling Indie in front of her family and friends, though I suspected he didn't care.

But Indie just grinned as she detangled herself from Linc, "We don't need a room, we have a whole freaking house!"

"Welcome home. All of you," Mrs. K said with a watery smile before turning away to make herself busy in the kitchen, her husband following close behind.

"Mum?"

"I'm okay. I'm just…" Mrs. K sniffled. "So happy to have you back."

"You sure?" Indie frowned, moving toward her mum, only to be held back by Nate.

"She's okay, In," he reassured her.

"Okay." Her voice was hesitant, and I thought I understood why. In the whole time I'd know the Kellermans, they'd never seemed overly emotional. They were posh and well spoken, perfectly presented at all times. They loved their children, that much was obvious, but they weren't big on displaying it.

Indie walked back to Linc. "Show me around?"

"Come on." He grabbed her hips and pushed her from the room, laughing as she twisted around and spoke in his ear.

"Glad to be home?" I asked Bailey, trying to ignore the fact that Nate was standing just behind her, but I couldn't. Not when I could feel his eyes on me. I ran a hand through my hair.

Do not look at him.

"Yes. I've missed this place so much."

I gulped down the last of my wine. "Really?" She missed Blackhill? The small seaside town with a population of barely two thousand people? There was nothing here.

I handed Kenzie my empty wineglass.

Do not look at him.

"This is where our family is," she replied, looking over her shoulder at Ryder. He caught her staring and winked before turning his attention back to his conversation with Nate.

I looked. I caved. I was weak. But I already knew that.

Indie's squeal of delight echoed through the cottage, causing everyone to turn in the direction it came from. Everyone but Nate and me. We were locked in a staring contest.

"Guess he showed her his hard—" Ryder grumbled as Nate, jaw clenched and still watching me, shot an elbow into his side in warning. "Work, finishing the studio." Ryder hissed out a laugh, holding his side.

He enjoyed tormenting Nate whenever they were together.

"Cake," Nate muttered. "Where's the damn cake?"

Cake? He looked away, and I sagged slightly, taking a deep breath.

"Nathaniel!"

"Sorry, Mum."

"Go and get your sister, and I'll get the cake."

"Ahh." Nate rubbed his hand over the back of his neck, his biceps flexing from the movement, drawing my eyes right back to the one person in the room I shouldn't have been drawn to.

Well, actually, that was a lie. There was no one in that house I should have been attracted to, enticed by. Why couldn't I meet someone who was not related to or friends with my ex-boyfriend?

"I don't really want to do that." Nate looked down the hall in disgust. "I wouldn't want to…actually, no! I will go and get her. It's her party. She should be out here with her guests." He sounded like he was giving himself a pep talk, like he had to convince himself to walk down that hallway and bring his sister back out, regardless of what she was or wasn't doing with Linc.

"Come on, you big baby." Kenzie grabbed him by the arm and dragged him down the hall in a show of moral support.

My heart lurched. It was stupid. Kenzie touching him meant nothing, but still I couldn't stop my heart from sputtering in my chest as they walked into the dark hall together.

Stupid emotions.

25

CHAPTER THREE

Nate

"Brody! Oh, my god! You're here too." Indie climbed onto the seat, jumped over Linc, and rushed for our cousin. We were back in the diner, the same one from the night before. Brody wanted to surprise Indie, so there we were in the booth at the back of the empty diner once again. But I wasn't complaining, because those burgers…

"Of course. Where else would I be?" Brody hugged her.

"Umm, at work or, you know, your home, maybe?" She climbed back over Linc and situated herself in the corner again.

"Didn't Nate tell you?" Brody pulled out a chair and sat down.

"Tell me what?" Indie glared at me.

"That I moved back to Blackhill?" Brody looked at me, and I shrugged.

Truth be told, I didn't tell Indie. And it wasn't because I didn't want her to know, but because I avoided all topics regarding Brody at all times. Hell, I avoided him as much as possible too. Not because I didn't like the guy. I did. We grew up together, and he was as much my best mate as Linc was. I avoided him because the guilt was too much to bear. Every time I looked at him, I felt terrible. So I tried to steer clear of all things Brody related. He hadn't noticed because he worked insane hours as a paramedic, or if he had, he'd not mentioned it to me yet.

"What?" Indie kicked me under the table.

"Ouch," I hissed at her before looking at Linc. "Control your woman."

Stupid mistake.

Linc laughed and shook his head like I should have known better.

I should have.

She kicked me again.

Hard.

"Dammit, Indie, that hurts."

"I am not his woman." She pointed at me. "And I can't be controlled."

"Clearly, you're a savage," I muttered and rubbed my shin where I was sure there would be blood streaming down if I chanced a look. "Linc didn't tell you either."

I was tempted to flip him off but figured the wrath of Indie would be enough punishment for how smug he looked when she mutilated my leg with her scuffed Chucks.

She spun to look at Linc with a raised eyebrow.

Linc raised his hands in defence. "Ace, relax. I didn't tell you because whenever I saw you, Brody was the last thing on my mind."

Indie smiled at him, satisfied with that answer. Linc slung his arm over her shoulder and flipped me off with the same hand.

Prick.

"But all those times you didn't see her and only spoke on the phone, you never thought to mention that Brody had moved back home?" I could have let it go, but I enjoyed messing with him too much. It was what we did.

"Seriously, In, I only moved back a couple weeks ago. Don't worry about it." Brody tried to diffuse the situation, but it was a futile attempt.

Indie spun in her seat and shrugged out of Linc's hold. "Why didn't you tell me on the phone?"

"Ahh, come on. Really?" Linc groaned and tilted his head back.

"Really."

Linc glared at me then kicked me under the table as well.

"Shit." Match made in heaven, those two. I rubbed my shin.

"Because when I spoke to you on the phone, Ace, Brody was the last thing I wanted to talk about," he said quietly, pinching her chin between his fingers.

That was my cue to close my eyes and not look at them.

Still too weird.

"Okay," Indie said softly. I peeled one eye open, and then another, and noticed she was back to sitting under his arm. "So where are you living?"

"At Nate's place." Brody reached for a menu

from the table behind him.

"Nate's?"

"Yep, ever since Linc moved out."

Linc had bought the old shack on the beach a couple of months ago and had been fixing it up for him and Indie to live in when she graduated. And Brody had moved back to town about a week before Linc settled the house and got the keys, so he slept on the lumpy sofa for a few weeks before taking over Linc's old room, while Linc moved out and finished renovating the home he planned on sharing with my sister.

Weird.

"Okay, good."

"You worried about my living conditions, Indie?" Brody teased.

"Just wanted to make sure you weren't living in some dive or sharing with some weirdo." She glanced at me. "Some other weirdo."

"Nope, all good. Nate needed a roommate to take Linc's place since you have him wrapped around your finger and buying you a house."

"I still can't believe you bought a house for us and kept it a secret from me," she said to Linc.

"It was bound to happen eventually. Sooner rather than later, don't you think?"

She dropped her voice to a whisper and put her lips against his ear so no one else could hear what she was saying.

Linc grinned. "Not now."

I shuddered.

Brody looked between us with an amused expression.

I didn't know what she said to him, and I didn't want to.

Too. Damn. Weird.

Bailey and Ryder took that moment to walk in through the doors, bringing with them howling wind and the rain that had begun to fall. The storm seemed to be settling in for the next few days.

"Julie." Ryder's face lit up as he dragged Bailey around behind the counter and gave the woman who served us last night a kiss on the cheek.

"Ryder, darlin', and Bailey, you sweet thing, good to see you back." She hugged them both before ushering them away with the promise of a round of Cokes and burgers on the house to celebrate their return.

Not one to complain about free food, I shoved the still unappetising menu aside and greeted Bailey and Ryder when they made their way over to the table.

"Kenzie coming?" Indie asked Bailey when she sat at the table next to us with Brody.

The booths were big, meant to seat six people, but it was too close for comfort. Bailey answered with a nod.

"And Harper too," Ryder said, falling into a tattered red pleather chair beside her.

Harper.

"Harper's coming?" Brody sat up and straightened his shirt. Ran his hands through his hair.

Linc looked at me with a raised eyebrow. And I knew what he was thinking. After reconnecting with Harper at my parents' wedding six months ago,

Brody realised his feelings hadn't quite gone away when they broke up. He was still trying to impress her and win her back.

"Yeah, she'll come join us as soon as she finishes work," Bailey answered.

After seeing her walk out of here last night, I wondered briefly if Harper worked here. And if she did, whether everyone else knew as well but decided it was not really any of my business. We weren't friends, even though she had dated Brody a few years ago when they were both in uni. We had only met the week of my parents' wedding when Kenzie asked if she could bring her friend along because she was scared of flying alone, and it just so happened Brody's ex-girlfriend was Kenzie's best friend.

"Is Kenzie bringing Cole?" Indie asked Ryder. "I miss that kid."

"Nah, it's too late for him." Ryder glanced at his watch. It was only six p.m. There was no way the kid would be asleep now. He was five.

Cole was Ryder's twin sister Kenzie's son, who also happened to be the son of Bailey's ex-boyfriend.

Yeah, their family was complicated.

Kenzie and Chace dated until she fell pregnant at fifteen and he demanded she terminate the pregnancy. When she refused, his family ran her out of town, and he moved on to the naive and unassuming Bailey before breaking up with her for Bailey and Indie's ex-best friend, Christina. The bloke was an asshole. And that was putting it nicely.

"Bailey, pretty lady. I heard you and the kid were back in town. I've missed seeing your face around here." I looked up to see a guy who I could only assume was the cook, judging by his greasy apron, hair net, and spatula in his hand, standing at our booth.

"Johnny." Bailey stood to kiss him on the cheek. "How are you?"

"Good." He smiled at her before glaring down at Ryder. "Don't get up on my account, kid," he said and slapped Ryder over the back of the head.

"I won't." Ryder punched him in the side.

"So, you guys know each other, then?" Brody asked.

Obviously, they knew each other. That would be why Ryder suggested meeting here and not somewhere...nicer.

"This little punk wandered in here about six years ago, looking like a lost and lovestruck little puppy. Caught the moron scratching his name into my tabletop with a sweet little love heart below it..." Johnny increased the pitch in his voice and wiggled his fingers in Ryder's face until Ryder slapped them away. "Never did get to finish writing who it was he hearted, but I think we can all guess whose name it would have been etched into my lovely Formica." Johnny winked at Bailey, and we all laughed, because Ryder had been in love with Bailey before she was even a blip on Chace's radar—another reason the guy deserved the award for the world's biggest asshole. "Forced the kid to pay for the damages, and turned out he could get his way around the kitchen almost—"

"Better," Ryder interrupted with a cough.

"Almost as good as I could. So, I gave him a job until the day he packed up and moved to uni with pretty Bailey, here."

"And the jerk never fixed the table," Ryder grumbled. "Made me work every day for three weeks with no pay and didn't replace the table."

"Taught you a lesson, didn't it?"

"No."

"What happened to the table?" I asked curiously.

"Nothing." Johnny reached into his pocket and pulled out a knife. "'Bout time he finished it off and wrote that name, I reckon." He handed Ryder the knife and nodded to the small table over by the front window.

"Just so you know, I'm not working for damages this time." Ryder snatched the knife from Johnny's hand before standing and kicking his chair back, with Bailey close behind, and walked over to the table he had marked with his name all those years ago.

Bailey stood back and watched as he scratched and carved what was clearly her name into the tabletop.

"Hey, Johnny," she called over her shoulder.

"Yeah, pretty Bailey?"

"I'm not working for this either."

Johnny laughed. "Noted."

Ryder finished carving Bailey's name and dropped the knife on the table before grabbing her by the face and kissing her.

"Told you this was real." He winked.

"Never doubted it." She smiled at him.

He picked up the knife and handed it back to a smiling Johnny. "Now, go back out there and make our food. I'm starving."

"Yeah, yeah. I might just spit in yours, kid." Johnny elbowed him in the stomach and called back to us, "Don't worry, I won't spit in yours. I save that for the VIPs."

"VIP doesn't mean what we think, does it?" Linc asked.

"If you're thinking it means Very Impatient Pricks, then you'd be right," he said with a laugh as he walked back to the kitchen.

"You guys are so gross." Indie screwed up her face at Bailey and Ryder when they sat back down holding hands and kissed again.

"You can talk...Ace," was all Ryder said, using Linc's nickname for her. Bailey laughed, and Indie blushed and shut up.

The door to the kitchen opened about fifteen minutes later, and out walked Harper with a tray full of burgers.

My jaw dropped. She did work here, and she was working tonight. For some reason, I assumed she worked with Kenzie at the hospital.

Brody's back straightened.

And Linc tilted his head curiously.

"Hey, guys." Harper set the tray of burgers on the table in front us.

Bailey and Indie smiled at her while Ryder lunged for the food.

Harper glanced at Brody and then me before muttering, "Hi."

She whipped off her apron and flicked her eyes

between the empty seat in the booth next to me and the lone chair at the table between Brody and Ryder.

I choked on air when she chose to sit beside me.

"Umm, how long have you worked here?" Brody asked, trying to sound casual, but I knew he was anything but. He had desperately been hoping for another chance for months.

"Since I moved back to town."

"Tell your uncle his burgers are still crap." Ryder smiled through a mouthful of food. So, he knew she worked here, which meant Bailey knew. And if Bailey knew, Indie knew. And if Indie knew...I looked at Linc, but he just raised his eyebrows and shrugged. He didn't know.

"He won't believe that, you know," Harper said, reaching for her own burger.

"But you know it's true." Ryder was cocky as hell.

"Your uncle?" I raised an eyebrow and reached for my own burger, wanting to know how bad they really were. Maybe last night was a fluke. Though I suspected it was just a long running joke between Ryder and Harper's uncle.

"Yep. Johnny is my dad's brother. I moved here with him and Julie about two years ago. Transferred my degree here and...yeah." She went silent and cast a nervous glance at Brody before she dropped her gaze to the table.

I got the feeling the reason she moved to Blackhill with her uncle wasn't something she talked about regularly. And I was sure whatever happened, Brody had no idea, judging by the

35

stunned expression on his face.

I took a bite of the burger and groaned. Ryder was wrong. They were still as good as last night. Best burgers in the state, for sure. "These are so good," I said, shovelling more deliciousness into my mouth.

"Wait until you try Ryder's burgers." Bailey nodded in agreement, a drop of sauce on her cheek.

"You've...ahh...got some..." I waved a fry in front of her face to draw attention to the fact she had sauce there.

"Thanks." She wiped it with her napkin and gave me a sheepish smile.

"Shouldn't we wait for Kenzie?" Indie asked, drawing attention to the fact that Ryder's twin sister still hadn't arrived.

"Nah, she'll be here when she gets Cole sorted."

Speak of the devil, and he shall appear. That was how the saying went, right? Cole took that moment to come rushing through the front doors. Unruly blond curls matted to his face from the rain and green eyes wide with fright, he lunged for Ryder as soon as he laid eyes on him.

"Whoa. Hey, buddy." Ryder wrapped him in a hug. At five years old, he looked the exact image of his uncle, only with lighter hair. "What are you doing here?"

"Mumma said I could come. She needs you." He sniffed.

"What's wrong? Where is she?"

"Outside." We all stopped to listen to the kid. What was wrong with Kenzie?

"Is she hurt? Cole, tell me what happened,"

Ryder urged, his voice laced with worry about his sister.

"No, she's okay. Just hurry, Unca. There's a man out there, and he wouldn't let us inside."

With that, Ryder passed his nephew to Bailey, who hugged him to her chest, and stood and stalked toward the door.

"It's okay, buddy. He'll bring your mumma inside," Bailey cooed in Cole's ear, rubbing her hand up and down his back to comfort him.

Linc looked at me with a slight tilt of his head. I nodded, and he stood, kissed Indie on the head, and followed Ryder out the door.

"Harper?"

She looked at me and waited for me to speak.

"Can you move?"

There was no way I was sitting in there when who the hell knew what was going on out there. But I knew one thing. I wasn't leaving Ryder alone out there with whoever was harassing his sister.

Harper slid out of the booth, allowing me to make my exit. I ruffled Cole's hair in reassurance as I walked past and heard Bailey whisper to him, "See, they're all going. It'll be okay."

Pulling my jacket tighter around me, I stepped through the doors into the howling wind and needle-like rain. Squinting in the darkness of the parking lot, I could just make out four figures on the other side, so I jogged toward them. Kenzie appeared to be screaming and yelling, but I couldn't hear her over the storm, and as I got closer, Ryder seemed to be struggling against Linc's hold.

Linc was arguing with Ryder, trying to hold him

back from beating the shit out of some dude who looked vaguely familiar. Kenzie was still screaming, and this time I could hear the abuse she was shouting at the Ken doll wannabe getting in Ryder's face.

"Kenz." I touched her shoulder, and she spun around so fast, her fist connected with my cheek. The crack of her knuckles on my bone echoed through the parking lot, even through the storm. Slightly disoriented, I shook my head and pulled her to me.

"Nate, I'm so sorry. I thought—

"It's fine. You hit like a girl," I laughed when all I really wanted was to ice my cheek because she hit nothing like a girl. "But you should go inside."

"I can't leave Ryder out here alone with him," she spat. The venom in her voice was jarring, and it dawned on me.

"He's not alone. Go to Cole," I said. "We've got him."

She looked over her shoulder at her brother, who was still fighting Linc's hold, and then to the diner where her son was inside worried sick about his mumma and his uncle. "Don't let him do anything stupid."

"Of course not."

"Thank you," she said and darted across the parking lot.

"Linc," I said standing just behind them with my arms folded and eyes narrowed on Barbie's boyfriend. "Let him go."

"What? No."

"Let him go."

Linc looked at Ryder and must have seen something in his eyes because he listened and let Ryder go, stepping back to stand beside me.

"It's him, isn't it?" he asked, folding his arms and watching as the fight unravelled in front of us.

Ryder was kicking his ass.

"Chace."

Chapter Four

Harper

No sooner had Nate stormed out of the diner in search of Ryder and Linc than Brody got up and followed.

"What is going on?" I asked the girls, but neither answered.

"I have a bad feeling about this." Indie pushed her food away and reached out to brush Cole's hair out of his face.

"Shh." Bailey glared at her then spoke to Cole, her eyes softening. "You hungry, buddy?"

"Can I have a burger?" Cole straightened, his eyes widening in delight.

"Sure."

"And fries?"

"Absolutely. Want a milkshake too?"

"Mum said I can't have chocolate or sugar before bed."

"I think it'll be okay. If she says anything, tell her it was my fault. Okay?" Bailey tickled Cole's stomach.

His laughter rang out through the diner.

"I'll go make you something special," I said to Cole, getting up from the booth. Bailey thanked me as I walked past.

It was nothing. The poor kid looked terrified when he walked in, so I was going to make him a monster chocolate shake with extra cream and ice cream. Whatever was going on outside, it couldn't have been good for them all to go storming out there.

As I approached the counter, the door opened, and Kenzie rushed in. "Where's Cole?" Her voice was panicked.

"He's okay," I said and nodded in the direction of the table where Bailey was drowning her fries in ketchup for him.

Kenzie touched my shoulder softly and hurried over to Cole, scooping him into her arms, and sat in the booth with him.

"He what?" Indie yelled. "Let me out. I'll—" She snapped her mouth shut after Kenzie said something to her, her eyes focusing on Cole, and she apologised with a wince.

"Harper, honey, everything all right?" My aunt came out to see what the commotion was.

I shook my head. "Can you make Cole a chocolate milkshake? Extra everything. I need to go make sure Kenzie is okay."

"Sure." Her smile dropped and her eyes narrowed, focusing on something over my shoulder. I looked behind me and gasped as she called out, "Johnny, you better get out there. Kid's gonna get himself in more trouble."

Nate was there. So were Linc and Brody. But it was Ryder who had my full attention. He had some guy by the scruff of his shirt and was punching him in the face repeatedly. Uncle Johnny came hurtling out of the kitchen and through the front, cursing as he went. Bailey, noticing Johnny's rush and me and Julie staring out the window, got up and ran out after him.

I wasn't sure what I could do, but I thought I should go out there and see what was going on.

"Harper?" Kenzie called.

"Stay there. I'll check it out," I urged her and followed Bailey outside.

Johnny shoved his way through the guys and was trying to pull Ryder off Chace. I knew it had to be him because she'd described him to me before and shown me old yearbook photos, and no one else could cause such a reaction in Kenzie or Ryder. Johnny was struggling to hold Ryder back as he swung his arms and kicked his legs in Chace's direction. He eventually broke free and lunged for Chace again.

Bailey ran around the guys and tried to insert herself into the middle of the fight, but Linc was quick enough to grab her around the waist and pull her back. Ryder was furious, and if she got in the middle, she'd likely get hit.

"What the hell is wrong with you guys, letting him do this? Let me go," she shouted and fought Linc's hold to get to her boyfriend.

I went and stood beside Johnny, who was still trying to call out to Ryder and get him to stop. Nate and Brody both tried, but each time they stepped close, Ryder shoved them out of the way. There was no stopping him. Good thing Linc held Bailey back. Ryder would never forgive himself if he accidentally hurt her. Chace danced on the balls of his feet, wiping the blood from his mouth as he tried to block Ryder's punches and get in a few of his own.

"Jones!" Bailey called out to Ryder, breaking his concentration for a moment and allowing Chace to get in one punch. And all that did was anger the already ferocious bull that was Ryder. He charged for Chace and knocked him to the ground.

"I swear to god, Lincoln, if you don't let me go, I'll hurt you," she hissed, but he just barked out a laugh.

"It'll be over soon. Just stay here or you'll get hurt." He tried to placate her, but it didn't work.

"One," Bailey said in warning.

"Bailey."

"Two."

"Don't be stupid," Linc argued.

"Three."

"Ow. Shit." Linc whooshed out a breath, let Bailey go, and pressed a hand to his side right where she elbowed him.

She crouched on the ground beside Ryder, who was preparing to hit Chace again, and touched his arm softly. "Jones, baby."

Ryder looked at her, the anger in his eyes dimming.

"Enough."

Ryder dropped his gaze to Chace—who was

almost unconscious.

"One more?"

Bailey watched him carefully for a moment and raised her hands in defeat. Ryder grinned and punched Chace one more time.

"It's like déjà vu," Bailey mumbled as she helped Ryder up.

"Great, kid. Thanks. What do I do with him now?" Johnny asked, curling his lip in disgust at Chace.

"Hell if I care. Leave him," Ryder said, throwing an arm over Bailey's shoulder. "I need to check on my sister."

"You might want to get Linc some ice for his ribs, though." Bailey smiled at Linc, who scowled back.

"What is with you girls knowing how to throw a punch better than us?" Nate chuckled, touching his cheek and following Bailey and Ryder back inside, with Linc muttering to himself.

"Bloody kid. He's back for one night." Johnny shook his head and leaned down to pull Chace up to a sitting position.

"I've got some gear in the car. I'll check him out and get him home," Brody offered dutifully and ran across the lot to his car.

"You wanna give him a hand?" Uncle Johnny asked me.

"Me?" My eyes widened in shock. That would be incredibly uncomfortable. After everything Chace had done to Kenzie and Cole, and Bailey and Ryder, the last thing I wanted to do was help him out. I was quite happy to leave him there in the rain

44

like Ryder suggested.

"You are the nurse."

"…sing. Nursing student," I reiterated.

"I don't want some little shit bleeding out in my parking lot. And don't you have to swear an oath to serve and protect or something?" Johnny raised his eyebrow at me.

"That's police officers." I folded my arms, just now feeling the sting of the icy cold rain on my skin.

"Just do it, or you're cleaning the grill for a month." Johnny sighed and walked away.

With his back to me, I stuck out my tongue and turned to face Chace, who was leaning against the wooden barrier of the parking lot with blood gushing out of his nose.

"I think he broke my nose again." His voice was thick and pained, but he earned no sympathy from me.

"You deserved it." I crouched in front of him and inspected his face. "How many times has he broken it now?"

"This would be the fourth." He winced when I pressed my fingers into his cheeks.

"You don't think maybe that says something about you?"

"No, I think Ryder has an anger problem."

I laughed humourlessly and intentionally put too much pressure on his swelling nose. "Does this hurt?"

"Ow, fuck. Yes," he hissed and swatted my hands away. *Good.*

"Ryder doesn't have a problem. You do. You

hurt everyone around you and don't care. All he's doing is protecting the ones he loves." I tilted his head to the side and inspected his face for any more cuts or possible broken bones.

"I do," he said softly, so softly I barely heard him through the wind.

"What?" I pressed my hands into his ribs to see if Ryder had broken anything there too, but Chace didn't even flinch.

"Care." He sighed and closed his eyes. "I do care."

"Yeah, right," I scoffed and stood back because Brody had returned with a small medical kit and began cleaning Chace's face.

"Why do you think I'm here?" Chace mumbled behind the cloth Brody was using to wipe away his blood.

"I don't know. To be a pain in everyone's ass? To cause more trouble and pain?" I tapped my foot impatiently, waiting for Brody to finish.

"I want to make things right."

I barked out a laugh. "A bit late for that, don't you think?"

"I can try."

Brody remained silent. I wasn't sure whether it was because he wanted to avoid any further disagreement or just didn't know the full story of how Chace got Kenzie pregnant at fifteen and told her to terminate the baby, and then went on to date Bailey and break her heart by cheating on her with her ex-best friend.

"Good luck," I muttered. There was no way Kenzie would forgive him, and Ryder wouldn't let him anywhere near his family again.

"He needs to go to the hospital and get his nose reset," Brody said as he packed away his things.

Great.

"You can drive him." I wasn't sitting in the car with him. "I'll follow and bring you back."

Brody nodded. "Let's go," he said to Chace and held his hand out.

"What?" Chace groaned and pushed himself to his feet.

"Your keys. I'm not getting your blood in my car."

Chace huffed and handed Brody his keys. "Watch the paint."

I shook my head and walked over to my car. He was such a douche.

CHAPTER FIVE

Nate

Kenzie was a wreck when I walked back inside. "Oh, my god. You said you wouldn't let him do anything stupid." She jumped out of the seat, a hard edge to her voice, leaving Cole sitting beside Indie.

"We didn't." Linc hissed in a breath and held his side as he slid into the seat next to Indie, who was frowning at him.

"What happened?" Kenzie asked and began inspecting Ryder's face.

"It's fine. I stopped him before he could kill Chace," Bailey answered because Ryder stood there with a smug look on his face, like it was no big deal, and he was probably right to give the guy a beating. I didn't know what started it, but I knew Chace deserved everything he got.

"And that's not stupid?" Indie nudged Linc in the side, causing him to jerk to the side in pain. "How is that not stupid? You know what he's like with Chace. And what happened to you?"

48

"Standing right here, In," Ryder growled while Linc shot a glare at Bailey.

She returned his look with a sweet smile and said, "I may have hit Linc. Just a little."

"You what?"

"Someone had to stop Ryder, and he," she pointed at Linc, "wouldn't let me go." She rolled her eyes and shook her head in disbelief.

Indie snorted. "Well, that was stupid."

"I didn't want her to get hurt," Linc defended himself.

"She won't. She's the only one who can calm him down and get him to stop."

"Yeah, kinda noticed that," Linc muttered and rubbed his ribs.

"Poor baby." Indie patted his cheek.

"Here, fix ya face." Johnny approached with a cloth for Ryder's bloody lip. It was amazing the guy still had any facial piercings left with the number of times he'd gotten into fights.

"Cheers."

"And ice your ribs," Johnny said to Linc, handing him some ice in a towel. "So, what the hell happened out there?"

Kenzie watched Cole thoughtfully, her eyes narrowing and a small frown on her face. "Nothing."

"Julie," Johnny called for his wife, "come give the little guy a tour."

Julie grabbed Cole and took him to have a look at the kitchen. "Let's go make something special for your mumma," Julie said to Cole, making him jump up and down in excitement as they left, talking about chocolate, strawberries, and pancakes. It gave Kenzie the chance to explain.

"Now, spill it." Johnny pointed at Kenzie and pulled out a seat. "Your punk brother is home for one day, and he's already getting into fights. I thought we were past this."

"I'm sorry, Johnny. Really. I didn't want this to happen." Kenzie dropped her head in her hands and slid into the booth beside Bailey and Ryder. "And I didn't want you to fight him." She looked up at Ryder.

"He deserved it," Ryder said, wincing. The cut on his lip looked pretty bad.

"He, who?" Johnny asked.

"Chace."

"The kid's dad?"

Kenzie sighed in response. "He wants to get to know Cole. Bailed us up in the parking lot when we tried to come inside. Scared Cole and freaked me out. I told him no and to leave because I don't even want Cole to know who he is. But we all know what Chace is like. He doesn't take no for answer."

"What's he doing here? I thought he was still at uni. His parents have gone. There's nothing in town for him anymore," Indie said.

"There's Cole," Kenzie answered.

"And why did you think it was good idea to beat the daylights out of him?" Johnny asked Ryder, who just smirked.

"Because he's a dick," he said in a matter-of-fact tone and shrugged.

"No arguments there," Bailey muttered.

"And you guys didn't think to stop him?" Johnny

looked at me and then Linc.

"Don't look at me." Linc held his hands up defensively. "I was holding him back. Nate told me to let him go. So I did."

Ryder reached his fist out for me to bump in a show of solidarity.

"You're all the bloody same. No more!" Johnny huffed, rubbing a hand over his tired face. "You gotta stop laying your fists into everyone who pisses you off," he said to Ryder then turned to me and Linc. "You gotta stop encouraging him." And finally to Kenzie, "You need to sort it out. Talk to him without Cole. Find out what he really wants, and if you still don't want him near the kid, get legal advice or your brother's going to end up charged with assault or worse."

We were all silent, letting the weight of his words crash down on us. Reality was a bitch, but he was right. It was time we all grew up and acted like the adults we were supposed to be.

"You're right," Ryder sighed. "But I can't make any promises when it comes to Chace and my family. Next time, I'll try not to hit him so much."

"Nex-next time?" Johnny leaped from his chair, knocking it over in the process. "There won't be a next time. I'm not bailing you out again, kid. This is my final warning."

Indie's eyes widened in shock and she bit her lip, looking at Bailey, who was just as alarmed as she touched Ryder's arm. His jaw clenched, his hands balled into fists, and he shot Johnny a warning glare that had Johnny backing up and cursing in apology.

"Okay. Okay. I get the last time. I do. But you

51

nearly…you know what? Never mind. Just no more. Please," he begged before turning and walking away. The last time? It had happened before?

"Someone care to explain what that was about?" Kenzie voiced the question that was swirling around in my head.

"Nothing. Forget it." Ryder looked at Bailey and leaned in, pressing his head to hers. It was an intimate gesture, and I shuffled my feet and looked anywhere but at them.

"No, I want answers. What was he talking about?"

"Dammit, Kenzie!" He slammed a hand down on the table, rattling dishes and toppling the salt shaker. I'll admit, I jumped a little at his outburst, but Bailey and Indie didn't appear fazed, like they'd seen this reaction before. That was kind of unsettling that they were so used to it.

"Don't 'dammit, Kenzie' me." She had to poke the bear, didn't she? She shoved her finger in his chest. "What was he talking about? You don't keep shit from me."

"One time. It was one time," Ryder said through clenched teeth, gradually calming down as Bailey wrapped her hands around his fists. Indie was right. She was the only one who could calm him down. I didn't know if that was a good thing or a bad thing.

"Ryder?" Kenzie urged, tapping her fingernails impatiently on the table.

Ryder groaned, tilted his head back, and squeezed his eyes shut, "One time. A couple of years ago, I just lost control. Ended up arrested and locked up until Johnny bailed me out."

"What?" Kenzie yelled. "How could you be so stupid? How could you not tell me?"

"It had nothing to do with you, Kenzie. And I'd do it again. He. Deserved. Everything. And more."

"What the hell were you thinking?"

"That I could make him suffer just as much as—" He shook his head, cutting himself short. "I'm not talking about it anymore. Chace got what he deserved. I got arrested, charged, and completed my community service and anger management classes. It's fine."

"Anger management?" Kenzie reared back, her voice a high-pitched screech. "What the hell, Ryder?"

I knew the guy was protective of his sister and Cole and Bailey, but I dreaded to think what Chace could have done that provoked him so much he ended up charged with assault and forced to take anger management classes. One look at Linc and I knew he was as clueless as I was. Indie knew, though. I could see it in her eyes, the fear and the sadness. Whatever happened, it was bad.

"Kenz, leave it, please," Bailey pleaded, her voice catching at the end. I was willing to bet it had everything to do with Bailey, judging by the look on her face. She was pale, her eyes wide with fright.

Taking a moment to think about it, Kenzie nodded and sighed in agreement. "I will find out one day."

"Kenz," Ryder growled, and she shut up, knowing not to push him further. I tilted my head and looked at Indie for an answer, but all I received was a blank stare. She wasn't going to say anything, at least not in front of Bailey and Ryder.

"Let's go," Ryder said to Bailey. "I need to get out of here."

"Okay," she replied softly, giving him a small smile.

"Sorry for ruining your first weekend home," Kenzie said as she stood to allow them out of the booth.

"You don't have to apologise for anything. Okay?" Ryder pulled her into a hug. "This is on me. And I'm working on it. But I better not see him around town again. I'm going to say bye to Cole."

He tugged on Bailey's hand and pulled her away with a wave to everyone.

"What—"

Indie held up her hand to stop me from asking the question we all wanted to know the answer to. "It's not my story to tell. Just know I would have been right there getting arrested with him if I wasn't with Bailey."

Kenzie frowned and lowered her head to the table. "This is so messed up. I thought things were going to get better, not worse."

"It will be okay. I promise," Indie reassured her. "We spent the last three years dealing with his narcissistic ass. He'll give up eventually and back off."

"At what cost? Ryder getting arrested again and locked up for longer? No, I need to sort it out now."

"Well, just remember you don't have to do it alone."

"Thanks, In."

Brody and Harper walked through the front door,

his hand on her back, gently guiding her over to the booth. My eyes narrowed, and my left one might have twitched too. They looked cosy. I wasn't jealous. I had no reason to be. It wasn't as if we were anything serious, and she ended things because it was the right thing to do. I'd be a pretty sucky cousin if I tried to move in on Brody's ex-girlfriend.

"Where were you guys?" I asked when Brody slid into the seat beside me, leaving Harper no choice but to sit next to him or at the other table.

Brody looked over his shoulder and glanced around the room.

"He's not here," Kenzie said, taking a deep breath, knowing he was looking for Ryder. "I better go and find Cole."

"Well?" I asked again. They'd been gone for a while.

"Dropped Chace off at the E.R. Ryder broke his nose."

Indie barked out a laugh but tried to hide it with a fake cough, sputtering, "Sorry. It's just he always breaks his nose."

"Four times, Chace told me," Harper said.

"Chace should have learned by now, particularly after la—" Indie snapped her mouth shut.

"After?" Harper asked.

"Nothing. The last three times Ryder has broken it."

"Is he pressing charges?" Linc asked Brody.

"Don't think so. He seemed..."

"Remorseful?" Harper offered.

Brody nodded.

"Remorseful. Ha. No. There's not a remorseful bone in that guy's body. He doesn't deserve anyone's sympathy. He needs to be lo—" Indie cut herself short again and groaned into her hands. "We need to go before I say something I'm not meant to."

"Okay, Ace, let's go." Linc slid out of the booth and pulled Indie with him, saying goodbye as they left.

And then there were three. We sat silently side by side in the large booth. It was awkward. No one knew what to say. I wanted to talk to Harper but couldn't with Brody there. Brody kept looking at me as though waiting for me to leave so he could have her all to himself.

"Well, it's been eventful. I'm going to check on Kenzie and Cole and then go to bed," Harper announced after a torturously long and uncomfortable silence.

"It's only seven-thirty." Brody glanced at his watch.

"I'm tired." Harper faked a yawn and waved goodbye.

"Guess we should go too, then, huh?" I asked Brody, shoving him out of the booth as he reluctantly agreed. The night was over before it started, but I had a feeling things were going to get a whole lot more complicated over the next few weeks.

CHAPTER SIX

Harper

Kenzie and Cole left minutes after everyone else. She was exhausted and freaking out, and it was making Cole anxious. I offered to let Cole stay with us for the night, and Johnny and Julie were happy to have him so Kenzie could calm down and have a break, but she refused, saying she didn't trust Chace not to come back and didn't want to let Cole out of her sight.

After everything I had heard about Chace over the years, I couldn't understand why he would suddenly show up here again and demand to know Cole. He had blatantly refused to acknowledge him and had caused so much pain and heartache for that entire family, Bailey included. It didn't make any sense. But Kenzie was smart and the strongest person I knew, so I was sure she'd get things under control sooner or later.

I walked Kenzie out to her car so she didn't have to cross the parking lot alone—that was how much

57

Chace had her riled up—and then went around the back of the roadhouse. It was still early, and even though I'd told Brody and Nate I was going to bed, I wasn't. I couldn't sleep, and I couldn't have sat with them in silence any longer. Nate looked like he wanted to say something, or maybe even stay, which was a bad idea. I couldn't be in his presence for too long alone because I didn't trust myself or my stupid hormones. And I wasn't willing to risk hurting Brody like that. Then I couldn't spend too much time with Brody either because the guilt of those three months with Nate weighed heavily on my chest.

There was this rickety old water tower in the field behind the diner. It was no longer in use and probably wasn't very stable, but the view from the top was incredible, so I ran through the field and the rain and climbed the ladder. I was soaked to the bone, but I didn't care. There was something freeing and calming about being out there in the storm, even if it was ridiculously dangerous, both from the slippery ladder and tower, and the strong wind. The moment I saw a flash of lightning, I was out of there, but until then, I'd enjoy the quiet and the view.

I settled back against the water tower and looked up at the sky. On a clear night, you could see the Milky Way, but tonight it was just black. No moon. No stars. Complete darkness except for the lights at the back of the roadhouse casting a soft glow over the field.

"What the hell are you doing up there?" I heard a voice shout, the sound almost getting lost in the howling wind.

It was probably Johnny coming to tell me to get my ass inside, so I scooted forward and peered over the edge. Jumping back, my heart in my throat, I smacked Nate in the chest as he climbed onto the platform beside me.

"What are you doing here?" I asked.

"Me? You're the lunatic sitting at the top of a water tower in the middle of the storm," he said, settling beside me and throwing a blanket over us.

I raised an eyebrow. "Where'd the blanket come from?"

"Johnny. I came back because I forgot my jacket." He wiggled around a little bit and fluffed the blanket.

"Doesn't explain why you're up here with a blanket." I couldn't help it. It was like my body acted on its own. I leaned in closer to Nate until we were shoulder to shoulder, hip to hip. Stupid girl.

"I asked where you were, and your uncle said you were out here. He threw the blanket at me and told me to take it to you so you didn't catch a chill and die."

"He's a little dramatic."

"He's not wrong. It's not exactly safe out here." He nudged my leg with his knee, and my heart skipped a beat. It literally stuttered in my chest from a simple, casual, and friendly gesture. I was screwed.

"Yet you're still here." I wrapped the blanket tighter around me.

"Can't have you freezing to death alone, now, can I? How would I live with myself?" Nate shifted slightly, his hand brushing my thigh.

"So, you're only here to save yourself the guilt later?" I squinted to look at his face.

"Exactly." He grinned, a big, wide, show-stopping smile, and wrapped an arm around my waist, causing a shiver to run up my spine.

I was *so* screwed.

Tearing my gaze from his lips, which were still smiling, I brought my knees up to my chest and thought of something to say, but I drew a blank

"You live here? At the roadhouse?" Nate asked.

"Yep, there's an apartment above the diner."

"And Johnny is your uncle?"

"He's my dad's brother." I nodded and hoped Nate wouldn't ask why I was living with my uncle and not my own parents. I didn't want to get into the family drama. They weren't worth my energy or my time.

"And you spend a lot of time up here?"

"Are you trying to bore me with small talk, or what?"

"Just making conversation." Nate laughed softly.

"Why?"

"Because you won't talk to me. But I figure if I talk to you long enough, I'll wear you down, and maybe we can be friends," he said thoughtfully. "Can we be friends, Harper?"

"Friends?" The word tasted funny in mouth. It didn't roll off my tongue as naturally as it did when I applied it to...any of my other friends.

"Sure. We're going to be seeing a lot of each other, I'd imagine, now that everyone is back. So, friends?"

"Okay," I agreed, even though I knew it wouldn't work. We could never be just friends. There would always be something more, something hanging in the background, lingering like the touch of his fingers on my skin.

Definitely screwed.

"Excellent. I've been in the market for a new friend since mine ditched me for my sister." He said it with such a serious tone that for a moment I was worried he might not actually approve of Linc and Indie's relationship, but then he laughed.

"You feeling lonely now?" I teased.

"Yeah, but you know, I've been keeping myself busy."

I frowned and bit my lip to stop from saying anything because a snarky comment about all the girls he'd been bringing home to keep himself busy was on the tip of my tongue. I couldn't let him know I was jealous, because I refused to acknowledge I was jealous. I had no reason to be. But when he smiled at me, and I imagined him looking at other girls that way, my heart hurt.

We were silent for the longest time until Nate finally broke it. "What are your plans this week?"

"We're making small talk now?"

"That's what friends do. They talk about small things. Or important things. You choose. I don't care. We can sit in silence in the freezing rain until our noses fall off if you want."

"I don't want my nose to fall off."

"Then why are we up here?"

"It's a good place to think, and the view is beautiful."

61

"Hate to break it to you, friend. We have no view." He gestured with wide arms at the darkness surrounding us. I couldn't hide the smile on my face from the way he called me "friend." If I wasn't careful, I'd get too comfortable with him and let my guard down. I couldn't let that happen. For his sake and for Brody's.

"Not tonight, but in the daylight or a clear night, it's pretty spectacular up here."

"Are you inviting me back?"

"What? No. I, umm…" I wasn't inviting him over again, was I? No. It was too much. Having him so close made my brain turn to mush and made me want things I had no business wanting.

"I thought we were friends."

"We are," I agreed reluctantly. Friends.

"And friends hang out at the top of water towers." He squeezed his arm around me. "You're shivering."

I hadn't even realised I was cold. "I'm fine." I was enjoying the warmth of his arm around me, and if I was honest, I didn't want to move.

"Come on. Let's get out of this rain. You can show me the view another day when the sun is shining."

Nate stood and held out his hand to help me up. I stumbled on the wet surface and slipped backwards, but he tightened his grip on my hand and pulled me forward into his warm, hard, very firm chest, his other hand sliding around my back to steady me.

"Whoa, you okay?" he asked, looking down at me.

I froze, unable to speak, and stared into his dark

as night blue eyes. All rationality was gone. Rain was dripping down his nose, cheeks, over his lips. His tongued darted out to lick the water away. My lips parted, and mimicking him, my tongue swiped over my bottom lip.

"Harper?" His voice was so soft as his head lowered so close to mine I was breathing in his breaths.

One kiss wouldn't hurt anyone, right? Right?

One kiss was nothing.

People kissed all the time, and it didn't mean anything.

It was harmless...

Only it wasn't. Nothing was harmless when it came Nate Kellerman.

"I'm okay," I said finally. The half a step I took back out of his arms almost physically hurt, but the daze he had me under was finally lifted, and I could think again.

A mask of indifference appeared on Nate's face, and he smiled as he rolled the wet blanket into a soggy ball. "Good. Can't have my new friend falling off a water tower."

Nate Kellerman was going to be the death of me.

CHAPTER SEVEN

Nate

"Sit down," Indie ordered and bounced on her feet with her hands behind her back while Linc stood beside her, quietly watching.

We were at our parents' house for Sunday night dinner—a new thing our mother was trying to implement now Indie was home and we were all living separately. It had been a week since I sat with Harper in the rain on the water tower, though I admittedly returned to the roadhouse a few times through the week, with the excuse that Johnny's burgers were so good I couldn't get enough of them, in the hopes of catching my new friend Harper. If I kept this rate up, I'd end up fat.

There was something about her that I couldn't shake. As hard as I tried to forget about her, I couldn't. I wanted her, plain and simple, and I shouldn't because I knew Brody did too. He talked about her all the time, wondering whether he should call her and see if she wanted to hang out, then second guessing his decision to call her because what if she didn't see him that way, and then what if she did. He was like a teenage girl, and he just kept going round in circles. Ordinarily I'd tell him to man up and ask the chick on a date just so he'd stop going on about it, but since it was Harper he was talking about, I'd kept my mouth shut. As terrible as it was, I didn't want him to have the opportunity for a second chance, not that I thought Harper would date him again because I was sure she wanted me the same as I wanted her. I just didn't want to risk it.

"What's going on, Indiana? Dinner will burn if you don't hurry up," my mother said as she perched on the arm of the sofa beside Dad.

"Well, we have something we want to tell you." She reached for Linc and pulled him close, his hands circling her waist and coming to rest on her stomach.

No.

Fuck, no.

"You better not have knocked up my sister, man," I growled and stood up.

"Sit down, son," Dad said and pulled me back into my chair.

"Relax, she's not pregnant." Linc held his hands up and shifted so he was standing beside her with an arm around her waist. I narrowed my eyes at him.

"But we are getting married," Indie announced holding up her left hand and flashing a diamond on her finger.

"And it's not a shotgun wedding?" I asked stupidly, but my mind was a little slow on the uptake. I stood up again.

"No, you idiot." Indie rolled her eyes.

"Oh, my baby's getting married." I was shoved to the side to make room for my mother to charge at Indie and Linc, wrapping them both in a hug and smothering them with kisses.

I shook Linc's hand and congratulated him when Mum finally let them go. He eyed me warily, still unsure whether I was actually okay with them together or if I'd murder him in his sleep one night. Sure, I was protective of Indie. She was my little sister, so it came with the territory, but if she was going to marry anyone, I was glad it was Linc. I knew she was safe with him, and he'd make her happy. In fact, they'd both been deliriously happy since my parents' second wedding in Fiji.

"I'm happy for you." I pulled Indie into a hug.

"Yeah? You're not going to go all big brother on me and beat up my fiancé, are you?"

"No."

"How did he propose?" Mum was gushing like a giddy schoolgirl.

"I didn't." Linc frowned. "I had it all planned out, a grand gesture, romantic and all that, but she beat me to it."

"Indiana, you did not propose?" Mum placed a hand on her heart in shock. She was a little traditional like that.

"I did. It just sort of happened."

"When?"

"Last week. On the way home, in the car." She laughed. "Very romantic."

"We wanted to tell you first before we

announced it to everyone else," Linc said, pulling two small silver envelopes out of his back pocket.

"What's this?" Mum twirled the paper in her hands.

"Open it and find out," Dad said.

I opened mine and slid out a small white card. It was an engagement invitation.

"You've already planned an engagement party?" Mum's eyes were wide, and she sounded disappointed.

Indie nodded. "We want to celebrate as soon as possible."

"But I can help plan the wedding, right? Because I'm good at that. Look at the second wedding your father and I had. We can hire Lavenia again, and she'll look after everything."

I groaned. I knew exactly what my mother would be like. She'd bulldoze the whole thing and plan it all to her tastes. It would be extravagant and over the top.

"Umm, well..." Indie paused and winced. "We just want something simple and small. And we're not in a hurry."

"But, you can't—"

"Leave it alone. If they want help planning their wedding, they'll ask." Dad placed a hand on her arm to calm her down.

"But—"

"Leave it alone."

"We'd love your input, Mrs. K," Linc said, nudging Indie in the side and shooting her a glare.

"Sure. It'll...be...fun," Indie said stiffly, forcing a smile.

"Oh, excellent. You won't regret this." She ran upstairs, muttering to herself.

"Oh, no! What have we done?" Indie whispered as she glanced over her shoulder.

"There goes your quiet wedding." I laughed and walked into the kitchen to grab a beer.

"I'll reel her in, sweetheart," Dad said, following me into the kitchen.

I handed him and Linc a beer, and Indie helped herself to some wine.

"Dinner is going to burn." She checked the oven and turned it off. "Where is she?"

"I'm right here," Mum announced as she walked into the kitchen holding a giant folder.

"What is that?" Indie eyed the folder that landed on the table with a thud.

"My wedding folder. Samples, images, contact phone numbers, websites. Everything you could need for a wedding can be found in here." Her smile was bright and wide, and her eyes sparkled with happiness as she flipped through the folder.

"How about we leave the wedding talk for another time?" Dad shut the folder and slid it out of her grasp. "I'm hungry, and you've worked hard on this meal. Let's eat and get through the engagement party before you start planning the wedding, okay?"

She agreed reluctantly, putting the folder on the counter and shuffling around the kitchen getting the food ready. Indie breathed a sigh of relief and gulped down her wine.

"You might want to look into eloping," I said quietly.

"It's crossed my mind."

"Say the word, Ace, and we'll go," Linc said.

"Really?" Indie spun to look at him.

"If that's what you want. It's your day, so you can choose." He kissed her head. Yeah, I was totally fine with their relationship as long as he kept putting her first.

"It's our day. You have to want it too."

"All I want is you to be happy."

"All right, you two, give the sappy crap a rest." I cringed and walked over to give Mum a hand, not wanting to witness any more.

Linc just laughed.

*   *   *

I was a sucker for punishment. Two days after Linc and Indie announced their engagement, I found myself at the roadhouse again, in the hopes of seeing Harper. After such a dark and depressing day, I really wanted to see her pretty smile and cute button nose.

"You look like crap and smell even worse," Johnny said when I walked in. I was beginning to like the guy. He was brutally honest. I knew I looked a bad and had definitely smelled better. The soot and scent of smoke was in my skin. It would take more than one shower to wash this day off.

"Yeah," I sighed and sat on a stool at the counter.

"What can I get you?"

"Tequila?" I was only half joking. He raised an unimpressed eyebrow and grunted. "A milkshake's fine." I slumped over the counter and rested my head on my arms.

"Rough day?" Leaning down under the counter, he pulled out a beer then flipped the top and slid it across to me with a nod.

"The worst."

"I'll get something to eat too," he said and pushed through the kitchen doors. "You got a visitor."

Harper peered around the door, her eyebrows pinched together. "Nate?"

"Hi, friend."

She rolled her eyes. "What are you doing here?"

"Wanted to see you."

"Why?"

"Because we're friends, and I had a terrible day."

She leaned on the counter in front of me, a look of concern mixed with surprise on her face. "And you came to see me? Why not Linc or Brody?"

"They don't have your smile. And I kind of need something bright to break through the darkness."

Her mouth pulled up into a smile, and pink tinged her cheeks. She ducked her head and tried to hide behind her hair.

"Walk with me?"

She nodded. "Hang on." She darted out to the kitchen and came back a few minutes later with a brown paper bag and two bottles of orange juice. "Let's go."

I drained my beer in a quick few mouthfuls and threw the empty bottle in the recycling.

I didn't know where we were going. The roadhouse was on the outside of town with nothing around for miles, but Harper seemed to have an idea, so I followed her.

"The water tower?" I asked as we rounded the back of the diner and began to trek through the field. Taking the brown bag from her hands and peering inside, I inhaled the scent of fried meat and potatoes and groaned, suddenly hungry.

"Not today."

We walked past the water tower and continued through the knee-high grass in the direction of a large willow tree at the back of the property. The sound of water trickling became louder the further we got from the diner, until finally we reached the shade of the willow tree on the bank of a stream.

Harper sat on a worn patch of grass and folded her legs underneath her.

"Come here a lot?" I sat beside her and leaned against the tree, closing my eyes only to open them again to stop the images flashing in my head, the screams echoing in my ears.

"Sometimes." She opened the bag and pulled out a burger and fries, handing them to me before digging back into the bag for her own.

We ate in silence, which was both a blessing and a curse. I didn't want to talk about my day. I didn't want to rehash the details and go over it again for the thousandth time. But in the silence, the thoughts crept in, plaguing my mind with doubt.

What if I did things differently?

What if I was there earlier?

What if? What if? What if?

Rationally, I knew there was nothing I could do, but it still didn't make it any easier.

It didn't lessen the guilt or the pain. Nothing

could ever prepare you for it. No amount of training and practice runs and theory could ever prepare you for death.

"Want to talk about it?" Harper asked, throwing her rubbish into the brown bag and moving to sit beside me.

"No."

She sighed and settled in against the tree trunk beside me, her long, milky white legs crossing at the ankles. She was the palest person I had ever met. Her skin almost glowed, it was so fair, yet her hair was so dark. Snow White—that was Harper, only edgier with skin-tight jeans and spiked leather boots.

"Want to walk again?"

"No."

"Swim?"

"No." Her questions barely registered in my distracted mind. In all honesty, I was content just sitting beside her as long as I didn't let my thoughts run away from me too much.

"Skinny-dip?"

"No." A tiny part of me wondered, if I'd said yes, would she have followed through and skinny-dipped with me in the stream?

"Want to make out?" She wiggled her eyebrows.

"You want to kiss me, friend?" I teased, grateful for finally getting my thoughts out of the cloud of smoke they were caught under, even if it only lasted a while.

"Will it cheer you up? You're worrying me." Her lips turned down into a frown as she brushed a hand across my cheek absently before jerking her arm

72

back as if realising what she was doing.

"Sorry. I dragged you out here because I had a really, really bad day, and now I'm being a terrible friend."

"You're not being a terrible friend. You're definitely not being a fun one, but I can understand that. Something happened at work, didn't it?"

I nodded. "How did you know?"

"You look and smell like you got stuck in a chimney." She rubbed her fingers across my forehead and cheeks, wiping away the soot that was still there.

"It was bad. The house was old and already fully engulfed in flames by the time we got there. We tried. So hard." I paused, needing to take a moment to get my head together again.

"Nate." Harper shook her head, at a loss for words, and reached for my hand, threading her fingers through mine. That was what I needed. Comfort. No words. Her touch. The warmth of her skin on mine.

"The screams. I can still hear them. A whole family, Harper. Trapped upstairs in that house," I ground out, my jaw clenched so tightly my teeth ached, but I barely noticed. "The smoke was so thick, we could hardly see."

Harper's hand tightened around mine while she wrapped the other around my waist and laid her head on my chest.

"The beams were falling down on top of us, the stairs crumbling beneath our feet every time we tried to take a step. We couldn't get to them. The ladders were no use. The moment Richie climbed

73

through the top story window, the floor beneath him gave out. There was nothing we could do." I choked back a sob, and Harper lifted her head to look at me, tears in her eyes. I wiped one away when it silently slid down her cheek.

"Eventually, our captain ordered us out. It was too dangerous, and he couldn't put our lives at risk. By this stage, the screams had stopped, and the fire was under control. There was nothing left of the house. We stood in the street and watched it collapse in front of us. They were dead. All of them because of a faulty air conditioner."

"Nate, I'm so sorry. I don't know what to say. How to make this better. Nothing is going to bring them back or take away your pain," Harper said, hugging herself to me.

"But she's alive," I whispered. I was still in shock. It shouldn't have been possible. No one could have survived that fire.

"Who? You just said they all...I don't understand."

"The girl. Can't be more than seventeen. I was outside talking to Brody. He was there, you know, to treat any victims and get them to the hospital. We were out in the middle of the road when I heard the cry. I was sure I imagined it, but it happened again. When Brody and I just looked at each other, I knew he heard it too. So we ran together into the falling-down house that was still smoking and hot to touch and searched everywhere. The captain was on the phone to the fire marshal and abusing the hell out of us for being in a dangerous building and ordering us out. We ignored him for a while and continued to look for her. We were just about to give up when we heard her again. Climbing over furniture and timber that was pure charcoal by that stage, we found her amongst the rubble in the bathroom, naked, burns to half her body, suffering bad smoke inhalation and part of the floor above holding her down."

"Oh, my god. How did she survive?" Her eyes were sad as she brought her hand to her mouth.

"She must have been in the bathroom when the fire started upstairs. It tore through the top floor so fast, and most of the damage downstairs came from the top floor falling in. Somehow the pipes in that bathroom hadn't been affected, and if it wasn't for the fact she covered herself in wet towels, she'd probably have died."

"What happened?"

"We wrapped her in the towels, careful not to touch her skin, and carried her out. Her screams were excruciating, and she kept writhing in pain. She passed out by the time we had her in the back of the ambulance. Brody gave her painkillers and sat with her as they rushed her to emergency."

"She's going to be okay?"

"Define 'okay.' She lost her entire family in that fire. But if you mean make a full recovery and live, then I guess…Yeah, she'll be okay."

"That poor girl. I can't imagine."

"You don't want to. She'll be in hospital for a while so they can treat her burns. Brody called on my way here to tell me."

Harper didn't say anything. Instead, we sat there holding hands and watching the water trickle over the rocks in the stream until the sun set and it turned cold. There was nothing to say. A young girl nearly lost her life today, and her entire family perished. And there wasn't a damn thing I could do to stop it.

CHAPTER EIGHT

Harper

Kenzie burst into my room the following morning. "Have you seen this?" she asked, waving an envelope in my face. I rolled over and buried my head under the pillow, completely uninterested in whatever it was that had her so excited.

"What?" I mumbled into my mattress.

"The invitation to Linc and Indie's engagement party."

They were getting married? I was happy for them, but I couldn't even muster the energy to fake excitement. I spent the entire night tossing and turning, my mind on Nate and what he'd told me about the fire.

"Did you hear me?" she asked. Why couldn't she just leave me alone and let me sleep?

I grunted out a response.

"Why are you still in bed?" The mattress dipped when she sat beside me. She pulled the pillow off my head and poked me in the cheek.

77

I swatted her hand away and grumbled, "Nate," not realising my mistake until it was too late.

"Nate?" She climbed over me and lay down beside me. "Well, this just got interesting real fast. Tell me more." She nudged me with her elbow.

"No. Not like that."

"Really? I've seen the lingering looks, and there was that one night in Fi—" I pinched her mouth closed to shut her up.

"Nothing happened."

"You woke up in Nate's bed with no pants! Something definitely happened."

"Kenz, please," I pleaded. I did not want to relive that moment because then I'd be forced to think about each and every other moment I ended up in Nate's bed without my pants. If that happened, I knew I couldn't be held responsible for my actions later, like if I just happened to lose my jeans and fall through Nate's window, only to land in his bed—completely not my fault.

"One day you will tell me what is going on."

"Nothing is going on. We're just friends."

"Best friends, actually," Nate said from where he suddenly appeared in my doorway with that heart-stopping grin. What was he doing here?

Kenzie's eyebrows shot up as I scrambled to rearrange the blanket and cover myself a little more, ridiculous as it seemed, given our history.

"Okay, well, I'll leave you to besties to, you know...talk." Kenzie winked and climbed off the bed, patting Nate on the chest as she walked past. She turned around and gave me a thumbs up before indicating to Nate and rubbing her chest. She either wanted me to rub my chest on Nate or wanted me to let him rub my chest. I wasn't sure, but either way, it wasn't happening.

"Just remember, Nate, she has class in an hour. So, make it good and make it fast." Her laughter could be heard all the way down the stairs.

"Sorry, I didn't mean to interrupt. I didn't realise she was here." Nate winced.

"That's okay. What are you doing here?"

"I don't really know. I didn't even realise I was driving here, but since I am, want to grab a coffee before class?"

"Ah, sure," I said and threw off the covers, completely forgetting I was wearing nothing but a t-shirt. "Let me just have a quick shower." I darted past him, only to be stopped when his fingers curled around my wrist.

Turning back to look at him, I saw his dark eyes were focused on something outside my window. He tugged on my wrist and pulled me to him. Releasing my wrist, he gripped my waist with one hand, bunching up my shirt exposing my underwear while he wove his other hand into my hair. It was a weirdly intimate moment and so intense my heart thudded against my chest.

His fingers skimmed the skin under my ribs, leaving a trail of goose bumps, while he tilted my head back to look at him, only he was still staring out my window. I leaned into him, both welcoming and hating the way my body responded to his closeness.

"You're wearing my shirt," he said in a deep, low voice.

79

"I...I—" I didn't know what to say. My brain had up and left. I only answered to his touch, which was leaving a blazing trail across my skin. I was wearing his shirt, one he left here one night more than three months ago. I had hoped he wouldn't notice.

"Raincheck on the coffee, friend?" he whispered, his lips grazing my forehead. "You've got a visitor right now, and I shouldn't be here." With one last lingering touch on my waist that turned my legs to jelly, he left.

A visitor? Who would be here, and how would he know? I stepped over to the window and peered outside. Dammit. Brody. What was he doing here? And how was Nate going to get away without being seen? Surely, he'd have seen Nate's car in the parking lot.

Deciding to skip a shower, I pulled on a pair of denim shorts, slid on my white canvas shoes, and tucked the shirt into my waistband at the front and ran down the stairs.

"Hey, man, what're you doing here?" Brody asked Nate as I rounded the corner into the diner.

"Uh..." Nate was caught, and he couldn't lie to save his life.

"Aunt Julie asked if he could stop by and take a look at the ice machine because Uncle Johnny is useless," I said smoothly, coming to stand between them.

"I heard that," Johnny grumbled as he came out of the kitchen. "There's nothing wrong with the ice machine."

"That you know of." I glared at him and pushed

him back into the kitchen before he could say anything to make Brody suspicious.

He walked off, mumbling something under his breath about damn kids not respecting their elders.

"I heard that," I called back through the door before standing in front of Nate. Perhaps a little closer than appropriate for a friend, but when it came to him, my body had a mind of its own.

"What are you doing here, Brody?" I turned to him, trying to act cool and like I was completely unaffected when Nate's fingers began playing with the hem of my shirt, twisting the back where Brody couldn't see.

"Thought I'd see if you wanted to grab a coffee," Brody said, his eyes bright, hopeful. What was with these guys and coffee? Two guys, two coffees, and I only wanted one.

"Oh, I'd love to…" I froze when Nate's fingers dug into the small of my back. A warning. "But I have class. I was just coming to see if I could take Johnny's truck today, because mine needs new tires."

"Well, that's easy. I'll give you a lift, and we can grab a caffeine hit on the way. After the hellish couple of days I've had, I need it." Brody's smile was so easy-going that it was hard to say no.

I didn't want to hurt his feelings and tell him to back off, even though I was absolutely not interested in him at all. No, I was completely invested in the guy who was trailing his fingers along the waistband of my shorts, unbeknownst to Brody standing directly in front of me.

"Ah, sure. Thanks." I forced a smile, even

though I would have much preferred to go with Nate. "Let me grab my stuff."

"Yeah." Nate cleared his throat, removed his hands from my skin, and stepped around me. "I'm off now. But tell Julie I'll be back tonight to look at the fryer."

"You mean ice machine?" Brody corrected.

"Whatever." Nate narrowed his gaze on me. "Tonight."

I stared, unable to form words because I knew it meant he was coming back tonight to see me, since there was nothing wrong with the ice machine or the fryer.

"See ya, man." He clapped Brody on the shoulder as he walked away, only to pause at the door and face us both again. "Nice shirt, Harper. Looks kind of familiar."

I ducked my head in embarrassment, the blood rushing to my cheeks. He just had to go and say that in front of Brody, who now stared at me in confusion.

"What's with the shirt?" Brody asked once the doors had closed behind Nate.

"Uh…it was Indie's. Guess that's why it looks it familiar," I said like a complete idiot, but I could hardly tell him it was Nate's. "I'll be two minutes."

I ran upstairs and grabbed my bag, throwing a few books in it, and quickly fixed my hair in the mirror. I don't bother to change my shirt because…well, Nate liked it, and I liked that Nate liked it.

Brody was waiting patiently when I got back downstairs. "Ready?"

"Sure."

We drove in silence to the university campus in the next town—it was practically a city compared to Blackhill. Brody gripped the steering wheel tightly. He fiddled with the radio stations, sighed, and rubbed a hand over his tired face. He was on edge.

"What's wrong, Brody?"

"How did you know?"

"I know you, remember." Nate already filled me in on what happened yesterday, but I wasn't about to tell him that. Because I wasn't prepared to answer the questions he'd no doubt have.

"Just wondering whether I am actually cut out for this job or not."

"What do you mean?" I knew the job was hard, but the reality was in this industry, people were going to die, and you had to be okay with that.

"There was a fire. A whole family perished, Har, except for one girl Nate and I found. It was horrible."

"I'm sorry, Brody." I reached over and rested my hand on his arm. A small comfort, but it was better than nothing.

He grabbed it with his own and squeezed my fingers. I wanted to pull my hand away. It felt weird. Our hands didn't fit well together, not like mine and Nate's. There was no spark, no tingle, no stutter in my chest, and that was the biggest sign of all. Brody and I were nothing more than friends.

"How's the girl?"

"Audrey? She's critical, but she should be okay."

"Audrey?"

"That's her name. I can't stop thinking about the

poor girl. She lost her entire family in the blink of an eye, and she's fighting for her life. Just wish there was something I could do." Brody pulled into the parking lot.

"I'm sure you'll think of something. You're kind, Brody, a good person. Even a visit would do you both good. You did save her life, and I'm sure she'd like to meet you."

"I doubt that. I saved her, but not her family. She has nothing now."

"Sure, she'll be upset, heartbroken, and devastated, but I'm sure she'd like to meet the men who rescued her. I know I would. She wouldn't be alive if it weren't for you and Nate."

"Maybe you're right." He tapped the steering wheel once and climbed out of the car. "Where's the best place for coffee here?"

I glanced around, taking in my surroundings, and tried to think of the best place to grab a hot beverage. Truth was, the campus cafés were severely lacking. Most coffee tasted like dirty water.

My gaze landed on a head of crazy, curly, blonde hair. Kenzie. But she wasn't alone. I couldn't see well from where I was standing, but I could tell she was worked up. She was waving her hands, and her voice, unintelligible but loud, carried on the breeze. Her left foot tapped the ground as she craned her neck and looked over her shoulder, moving just enough to give me the perfect view of who she was talking to.

"Shit."

"What?" Brody asked, but I ignored him and

rushed over to Kenzie.

"Kenz." I reached her and placed my hand on her back.

"Just go, Chace. I already told you no."

"You can't stop me. He's my son. I have a right to see him."

"You have shit. You lost that right when you ordered me to abort my child. What kind of person does that?"

"I was fifteen, dammit. A kid."

"So was I," Kenzie growled and took a step forward, but Brody appeared out of nowhere and pulled her back.

"My parents were furious. Threatened to cut me off. What did you expect?" He ran his hands through his hair. He had a plaster over his nose, and his eyes were still black with bruises.

"Yeah, great. Sure, that'll be a huge comfort to Cole when he cries to me at night wanting to know why his daddy doesn't want him."

"But I do. Why won't you let me see him?"

"Because I don't trust you. You'll be the best thing in his life for three months, until something more interesting catches your attention, and you disappear without a word. It would break his fragile little heart, and I'm not willing to risk that." She took a deep breath, still held back by Brody's hand on her arm. "I know you, Chace. You only do things if it's good for you. And having a child is not good for *you*. Your life becomes about them. Having a child means everything you do, you do for your child. They always come first, not as an afterthought. And to you, Cole is nothing more than

85

an afterthought. A way to piss off the parents. A way to pass the time. But to me, Cole is my entire life. I live for him, and I'm not letting you fuck with that."

Chace stood there, stunned, at a loss for words for a moment before setting his gaze on Brody. "And who's this? Some dude you've got pretending to be the kid's father?" he scoffed.

I winced and waited.

"The kid's name is Cole. And you wonder why I won't let you near him. You're petty and jealous and can't even say his name."

"Let's go," Brody suggested quietly.

"Kenzie, we're not done here."

"Yeah, we are," she said. "Back off."

Kenzie nodded to Brody and turned away from Chace. We walked together, ignoring Chace's calls to come back, toward our first class with Kenzie muttering to herself the whole way. He was really screwing with her head. "How did he know I was here?"

"I don't know." I had to admit, it was weird that he knew what uni she attended and where she would be. Had he been waiting for her long? Or did he know her entire schedule?

"Is he stalking me or something?"

"I wouldn't put it past him."

"Want to see if I can find out?" Brody offered. Damn, I forgot he was still there, but at least this saved me from sitting through an awkward coffee with him.

"How?"

"I know a few guys on the force. Could get them

to check him out."

"You would do that?"

"Sure."

"Thank you." Kenzie leaped forward and hugged Brody. "Should I come with you?"

"If you want to." He smiled.

"Now?" Kenzie pressed. "I don't want to stay here knowing he could still be waiting after class."

"Uh…" Brody looked at me for an answer, so I shrugged. It made no difference to me if they left now. I could lend Kenzie my class notes later to catch up. "Sure."

"Oh, crap. Harper. How will you get home?" Kenzie turned to me as if suddenly remembering I was there.

"I'll be fine. I'll get a ride with a friend."

"A friend?" She raised her eyebrow at me and pursed her lips. "You don't have friends."

"I do so." I folded my arms and frowned. "I have a new one."

"Oh, really?" Her eyes twinkled as she realised I was referring to Nate. "A new bestie, huh?"

"If you're not careful, then yep. I'll replace you. Go. I'll be fine."

"Okay. Thanks, Harper." She hugged me briefly and stepped back.

"Raincheck on the coffee?" Brody asked. I groaned inwardly. I had already heard that today.

"Sure."

"See ya."

I waved and watched them walk away together. Kenzie turned around, continuing to walk backwards. "Make sure you and your friend are safe. Use protection and all that."

I ground my teeth and glared at her, but she just winked and continued. "Seatbelts, Harper. I don't know how good a driver this friend of yours is. Are they good? Know what they're doing?"

I thought about my response for a minute before deciding and calling out, "The best." I winked. Her mouth dropped open and her steps faltered before she gave me a thumbs up and turned around again. She was going to ask a thousand questions later, and I'd have to come clean.

CHAPTER NINE

Nate

I slammed my fist into the steering wheel when I pulled into the driveway of The Love Shack to see if Linc wanted to go for a surf. I needed to clear my head and calm down.

Therapy sessions.

What a load of bullshit. I didn't need therapy sessions, but Cap said it was mandatory for all of us after that disastrous fire. I argued with him until I was blue in the face, but ultimately, he won because it was either complete the sessions or he'd suspend me indefinitely.

Walking in the back door, I called out to see if anyone was around. Indie's voice travelled through the cottage from her studio. "In here."

I found her sitting in a white wicker chair, a sketch pad and charcoal beside her and her phone pressed to her ear. She smiled when I walked in and held up her finger to tell me she'd only be a minute.

"I miss you too."

I had no clue who she was talking to. Linc, maybe? Because he was nowhere around, but telling him she missed him was a bit much since they lived together.

"When are you getting here?"

I wandered around the studio, looking through all her art supplies and some of the paintings and drawings she'd already done. They were all of the beach and Linc. Of course.

"You've got a break for the next couple of months until the semester starts again. Stay for the summer. It'll be fun."

Paint drops already decorated the whitewashed floorboards. She'd well and truly settled in. Give it a few months, and I was sure the entire room would be coloured like a rainbow.

"Yes! Of course." Indie bounced in her chair, a wide smile on her face.

I took a seat in the chair beside her and reached for her sketch pad. She slapped my hand away and narrowed her eyes, not wanting me to see what she was working on. I grabbed it anyway and flicked it open to the piece she was in the middle of before talking to whoever was on the phone. The beach, waves, and what looked like the beginning of a person out in the water. Looking out the large window at the ocean, I spotted Linc in the distance paddling back out over the break. She was sketching him while he surfed.

How romantic?

I gagged, and Indie slapped me.

"You can stay here or with Ryder and Bailey. There's plenty of options." She paused while the other person said something. "Really?" Her face lit up as she squealed with excitement. "Okay, I can't wait. See you then." She dropped her phone onto the table beside her and snatched the sketch pad from my hands.

"Don't touch."

"You're drawing Linc?"

"He's my muse." She shrugged.

"Who was on the phone?"

"Jack!"

"He's coming here?" I leaned forward and rested my elbows on my knees.

"Yeah. He's bored and lonely. And he doesn't go back to school for a month or two, so I figured why not invite him for the summer. He was coming for the engagement party anyway."

"Fair enough." I stared out the window and watched Linc surf.

Indie was quiet.

"What's up?" she asked after a while.

"Nothing."

"You look exhausted."

"Didn't sleep well, and work's just…busting my balls. They want me to go to therapy after yesterday."

"Yeah. Sorry. I heard about that. So, go."

I took a deep breath. It wasn't that simple. I didn't want to talk about it. I didn't want to talk about my feelings. I just wanted to forget it happened and move on. Why couldn't people leave well enough alone? I was fine. "I don't need to."

"Why didn't you sleep well?"

"I kept hearing the screams and seeing the girl

91

curled in a ball on the floor waiting to die."

"Uh-huh." Indie had her arms crossed and her head tilted to the side and worry in her eyes.

"What?"

"You need therapy."

"I don't. I'm fine." I ground my teeth.

"You're not. If you were fine, you would have slept last night."

"Whatever. Cap says I have to go or I'm suspended."

"So, what's the problem? You don't have a choice. Go, get it over with."

"I hate talking about that. Feelings and stuff."

"It's better than bottling it up."

"Whatever. I'm going for a surf." I stood and walked out of the room, leaving Indie there in silence.

I grabbed one of Linc's boards from beside the back door and jogged down to the beach where I dumped my clothes, only keeping my shorts on, and paddled out to where Linc was sitting on his board, waiting. The water was freezing. It wasn't near hot enough to be out in the water, but it was peaceful, and that was what I needed.

"Hey, man," he greeted, narrowing his eyes at the hard expression on my face. "Ready?" was all he asked. He knew me well enough not to demand answers or tell me what to do. He'd surf with me until I calmed down.

I didn't know how long we surfed, but I was still on edge. I was still thinking about the girl in hospital fighting for her life. I could still hear the screams of the family crashing over me with the waves.

My thoughts drifted to Harper. Sitting under that tree with her last night, having dinner, it was good. After telling her about the incident, I barely gave it a second thought. She made it easy to forget.

I needed Harper.

And that was only going to end in trouble.

But I didn't care. I needed to see her. Talk to her. If only to silence the screams in my head.

I told Linc I was done and paddled back to shore, ignoring his calling me back. I grabbed my clothes off the sand and returned Linc's surfboard as quietly as possible so Indie didn't hear me and want to talk.

I didn't bother getting dressed. I was still dripping wet, and there was nothing worse than wearing dry clothes when you were wet. Once in the car, I pulled out my phone to call Harper, only to notice three messages from her.

The first one was sent two hours ago.

Harper: Hi, friend. I have a favour to ask…

I smiled at her calling me "friend" and read the next one, sent only minutes after the first.

Harper: Any chance you could pick me up after class? Long story, but Kenzie left with Brody, and she's my ride.

Dammit. What time did she finish class? And why the hell were Kenzie and Brody leaving together?

Harper: *Okay, never mind. I guess you're busy. I'll just walk.*

That one was sent fifteen minutes ago. She couldn't walk. It was a thirty-minute drive, at least. It'd take all night to walk. I started the car and pulled out of the driveway while fumbling with my phone.

"Hello?" she answered after a few rings.

"Where are you?"

"Nate?"

"No. It's Santa Claus."

"Very funny."

"Where are you?"

"Waiting for the only cab in three towns to pick me up." She sighed. That was the thing about small towns—transport options were limited.

"Where?"

"By the pier. I walked that far and gave up."

"Wait for me. I'll be there in fifteen."

"Fifteen? Where are you?"

"Just left Linc and Indie's."

"I'm sure the cab will be here in a minute. It's fine. Don't worry. You're at least half an hour away. I'll just catch you later."

She didn't get it. I needed to see her.

"I'll be there in fifteen," I growled.

"Nate, don't do anything stupid, okay? Relax, slow down. I'll wait. But I want you here in one piece."

"See you soon, friend." I hung up and put my foot down a little harder.

True to my word, I pulled my car into a parking

spot by the pier fifteen minutes later.

Harper was sitting on a bench facing the water when I approached and sat next to her.

"Hi," I said.

She turned away from me, leaving me to stare at the small red poppy tattoo on the back of her neck.

"I don't get a response?" I wondered what I had done wrong. I drove all the way out there to pick her up so she wouldn't have to rely on a cab which would have cost a fortune, and she wasn't talking to me all of a sudden. What could have changed in fifteen minutes?

"No," she said, her voice cracking.

"Harper?" I touched her shoulder, but she shook me off. "What's wrong?"

She sniffed and brought her hand up to wipe her...nose, face, eyes? I couldn't tell because she wouldn't look at me. I stood, walked around, and crouched in front of her. She lowered her head.

"Talk to me, please?"

"You're an idiot. A complete fool." Her voice was hard as she pushed me away with such force that I fell backwards, catching myself with my hands and sending shooting pain through my wrists from the impact.

"What did I do?" I rose to my feet and dusted off my hands. Why was she so angry at me? A cab pulled up at the side of the road.

"Fifteen minutes, Nate!" She jumped off the bench and shoved me again. "Do you know how stupid that was? How irresponsible? Huh? Did you think about the consequences?" She grabbed her bag from the ground and stormed off toward the waiting cab.

I chased after her and pulled her away from the door she'd just opened. Leaning in, I told the driver to leave.

"Whatever, man." The guy behind the wheel shrugged and drove off as I slammed the door shut.

"I can't believe you," she shouted. "Just go. I'll find another way home."

"No." I grabbed her arm and pulled her to me. "Not until you tell me what I did."

"You don't get it, do you?" she cried and beat her fists against my chest.

Dammit.

I wrapped my arms around her and rubbed my hand up and down her back. She struggled against me, wriggling in my arms, attempting to free herself from my hold, but I wasn't letting go.

"Not if you don't tell me."

I got here in the time I told her I would. It was a little faster than it should have been, but I only did that because I had to see her, needed to see her, and I didn't want her waiting around by herself or getting into the car with someone she didn't know. And then it hit me. She told me to take my time, and I didn't.

"I'm sorry. Okay? I shouldn't have sped here like that. I just wanted to see you. Make sure you were safe," I whispered to her as calmed down.

"But that's just it," she said so softly I strained to hear her.

"What?"

"You were so worried about me that you didn't care about yourself or anyone else." Her hands

96

gripped my shirt as her tears soaked through to my skin. "What if something happened?"

"But it didn't. I'm okay. You're okay. It's all okay."

"It's not, and I'm not."

We were still standing on the curb, so I walked her—still wrapped in my arms and against my chest—to the bench and sat, pulling her onto my lap.

"Something happened, didn't it? To you or someone you care about." I tilted her face up and brushed a strand of black hair from her eyes. It was the only thing that made sense. The only thing I could think of that would cause her to react that way.

She nodded.

"Want to tell me about it?"

She shook her head.

"I'm sorry," I said again and wrapped my arms around her, holding her close.

Eventually her sobs stopped, her breathing evened out, and her tears dried. But neither of us moved. Neither of us spoke. We just sat with her curled in my lap and my hands rubbing soft circles on her waist.

"My brother," she said after the longest time. Her voice was raw and scratchy, full of emotion. Full of sadness.

"What happened?"

"He killed someone."

I flinched. I didn't mean to but that was a huge bombshell to drop on someone. She noticed and tensed in my arms as though preparing to get up and walk away. So, I did the only thing I could think of and pulled her closer, letting her know I wasn't going anywhere. I wasn't judging. I was just listening.

CHAPTER TEN

Harper

I sighed. I hadn't talked about what happened with my brother for eight years, since I stopped going to therapy, and I didn't know how to talk about it now. But I wanted to. Something about Nate made me want to tell him everything. Kenzie didn't even know, and Brody had no clue. For the most part, I blocked it out as much as possible, choosing to ignore the nagging in my head to dredge up old memories I'd rather forget. Memories that made my heart hurt.

"Nine years ago, my brother killed someone. A kid. Same age as me. Thirteen." My voice trembled as I spoke. Nate stiffened and inhaled sharply but didn't speak. Hearing someone killed anyone was a shock, but hearing someone killed a kid was hard to understand. "My parents were the lowest of low. They were addicted to everything. Alcohol, cigarettes, drugs, gambling. You name it, they did it. Life sucked growing up, and my brother was my guardian angel." I smiled sadly at the thought of my brother, who I'd not seen or spoken to for two years. The one who told me to go and not come back. The one who abandoned me for my own good. I missed his smiling face, and the way he used to take care of me.

"One night, I-I can't really remember the details. I've blocked a lot out, but my parents used to drag me around everywhere with them. I was young, innocent looking, so they'd send me into their various dealers' houses or drop me off on street corners to buy their drugs while they circled the block and came back. No one was going to suspect me of doing anything like that. I was the perfect cover."

Nate growled and tightened his arms even more around my waist, pulling me into the safety of his embrace. The beat of his heart echoed mine, erratic and unstable.

"Anyway, this night they took me to a…I guess you could call it a party. I'd left my brother a note in our secret spot. We didn't have phones then, so we left messages to each other under a loose floorboard in my room. He was working, but he would be finished soon. He was always working. Trying get enough money together so when he turned eighteen, he could get me away from them. I followed my parents into this house. It was putrid. The walls were stained yellow from cigarette smoke, there were bloodstains on the carpets, and everything else was black from dirt and grime, used needles littered the floor and countertops and everywhere."

I took a deep breath, needing a minute compose myself. Nate's head was buried in the crook of my neck, and he still didn't say a word. His hot breath drifting over my skin was comforting, and in that moment, I felt cherished, calm.

"They were high. Like always, but it was wearing off. They were always looking for their next hit, chasing that high. As terrible as it sounds, I liked them better when they were high. They were always too out of it to pay attention to me when they were smashed. It was when they were coming down that life got…hard." I swallowed the lump in my throat, forcing the tears back. "So, they were coming down, but you know, their dealer was right there. The goods were on the table. Only they didn't have the cash to pay. They were begging, pleading, offering anything for just one more hit, but h-he…he wasn't interested. He didn't want their car. He didn't want my mother." I laughed bitterly. "Yeah, she offered herself, and he turned her down. He wanted one thing, and one thing only."

Nate's fingers dug into my skin, pinching, hurting, but I welcomed the pain. It took away from the pain in my chest, gave me something else to focus on.

"Don't. Say. It." His voice was rough, broken, his lips brushing against the top of my shoulder and sending a shiver up my spine. Such a sweet yet innocent action had the power to break me and put me back together at the same time.

I nodded and bit back a sob.

"Me. He wanted me. I was thirteen. As messed up as they were, I was their daughter. They loved

101

me in their own way. They wouldn't allow that. They wouldn't do that to me. But they did."

"Harper?"

Tears were rolling down my cheeks, but I didn't stop them. I needed to finish the story. He needed to know everything. "I don't remember what happened next. I blocked it all out. I only know what the police told me after. Someone in that house, I don't know who. I never asked. Someone dragged me out of the house be-before things got too far. My clothes were torn to shreds, but I wasn't harmed. Whoever it was saved me."

Nate breathed a small sigh of relief and pressed his lips to the side of my neck, soft and warm. I settled into his arms, trying to lose myself in him.

"I was taken from my parents and put into foster care the next day. But my brother, when he got my note about where my parents were taking me that night, he jumped into his car and came to find me. Only he didn't make it. He was so out of his mind with worry, all he wanted to do was get to me. It was dark, and the road was wet. A kid from my school crossed the road, came out of nowhere, and Jeremy…my brother was driving too fast. He didn't see him until it was too late. He couldn't stop in time. In one night, I lost everything. I lost myself and my brother. He was jailed for involuntary manslaughter and reckless driving."

"Shit." Nate took my face in his hands and turned me to look at him. The pain, the sadness, and the worry were all there in his eyes. "Harper, I—" He pressed his forehead to mine.

He was at a loss for words. Understandable,

given all the information I dumped on him. I didn't need him to speak. I just needed him to understand my reaction earlier. I needed his warmth and safety.

"He was given ten years and was eligible for parole after eight."

He pulled back slightly with wide eyes. "So, he's out?"

"I don't know. It's been two years since I last spoke to him. He ordered me away. Told me to make something of my life, not spend every other moment speaking to him behind a glass wall. He didn't want me to wait. He didn't want me to see the way prison changed him, hardened him. He-he…" I was losing it. My brother was my whole life, and he refused to see me again. I tried for weeks after he sent me away, but each time was told the same thing, "Jeremy Donovan is not taking visitors," so in the end, I gave up. I tracked down an uncle I'd never met and packed my bags. That was how I came to live in Blackhill with Johnny and Julie.

"Shhh," Nate whispered, staring into my eyes. Wiping the tears from my lashes and running his hands through my hair, he brought my face impossibly closer to his. I reached up and placed my palms over his, weaving our fingers together, not wanting to let him go.

"It's okay. It'll be okay," he said, his lips barely brushing mine as he spoke. "It's okay." He repeated the words over and over. Our breath mingled, and our lips grazed each other, but that was it. He didn't try to kiss me, and I didn't try to kiss him, though I wanted to. So bad. I was content. He was reassuring. "And your parents?"

"Dead, for all I know. Haven't heard from them since that night. Uncle Johnny refuses to acknowledge that my dad is his brother and never speaks of him."

Nate pressed a kiss to my forehead and tucked me under his arm again.

We sat and watched the waves crashing against the shore until the breeze cooled and the sun began to set. We'd not moved or spoken for hours, each of us lost in our own thoughts, and neither wanting to let the other go. I knew this because every time I shifted positions, Nate would tighten his hold on me, bringing me closer to his warmth.

"We should go," he said and pressed his lips to my temple.

I closed my eyes and smiled. "Not yet," I said, making no move to leave his embrace.

"Why?" he asked, dipping his head to my shoulder again.

"Because I like where I am right now. It feels right, and I don't want to lose this feeling," I said honestly, because against my better judgement, I was at risk of falling for Nate Kellerman.

Nate trailed his nose across the top of my shoulder and up the curve of my neck to the sensitive spot behind my ear and whispered, "I don't want to either."

I was wrong. I wasn't at risk of falling. The figurative ledge beneath my feet had already given way, and I was falling. Hard and fast. It was out of my control now, and all I could do was hope to survive.

"But," he continued. One word, and it was like a bucket of cold water was dumped over my head. I jolted in his arms and jumped to my feet, taking a step back. "You said it yourself. We can't do this."

I folded my arms and nodded.

Rejection wasn't enjoyable. At all. Even though it was right, it didn't feel it.

Nate reached for me, his fingers gripped my hips and pulled me to him. Leaning his head against my stomach, his fingers splayed on my sides, he spoke again. "The consequences. Brody. It's not fair to him."

I dropped my arms and threaded my fingers into his hair. Hearing him repeat my words was like a kick in the gut. Was that how he felt when I first ended things? Letting out a frustrated breath, I knew he was right. I was right. It just wasn't fair. No one had made me feel this way. No one had made me care this much, not even Brody. Not the way I cared for Nate. I had never wanted anyone more than I wanted him, and I just wanted to say…

"Screw the consequences."

Nate pulled back, his head lifting to meet my gaze. His eyes were dark, calculating as he chewed on his lip, contemplating my words.

"Harper…" he warned.

"Nate."

He pushed me back gently, releasing his grip on my waist. "I'm going to hate myself for this. You're going to hate me too. It can't happen. It's not right." He stood and picked up my bag from beside his feet.

He was wrong. I didn't hate him. I couldn't hate

someone for doing the right thing out of love, concern, and respect for another person's feelings. But I could up my game and make him surrender. I wordlessly slid my hand into his, entwining our fingers, and walked beside him toward the parking lot. He opened the car door for me but stopped me before I climbed in. My back was hard against the window, but Nate leaned into me, his hips pressing into mine and one arm braced against the car while the other cupped my cheek.

"Thank you," he murmured. "For trusting me and telling me your story."

And then...

He kissed me.

I gripped his shirt and pulled him closer, but his mouth remained closed. Clamped shut. There was no movement. His tongue stayed firmly behind his lips. It was nothing more than his mouth on mine. It was a kiss that said everything. A kiss that said he wanted to kiss me but couldn't. A kiss that said we were more than friends when we couldn't be. A kiss that said he wanted me as much as I did him, but it could never happen. A kiss that said we were just friends, when neither of us wanted that. It was a kiss that felt like the end before it even began.

"Let's go...friend," he said and stepped back to let me in the car.

We drove in silence all the way back home, my lips aching and tingling to feel his again. My fingers tangled with his and rested on his knee. My heart held firmly in his tight fist clenching the steering wheel.

CHAPTER ELEVEN

Nate

I stumbled into the kitchen to make coffee. My eyes were dry, scratchy, and burning, and my lids were heavy. I was exhausted. Lack of sleep did that to a person.

"What the hell, man? You're a wreck," Brody said as he threw the paper down on the table on Monday morning.

I ran my hands over my face and fumbled with the coffee machine. I didn't want to talk about it. I was tired, cranky, and needed coffee.

"What's going on?" he pressed and came over to put his breakfast dishes in the sink.

"I didn't sleep well last night." I grabbed a mug from the cupboard and almost dropped it.

"It wasn't just last night. Was it?" Brody leaned against the counter and watched me.

"What do you mean?"

"Thin walls. I hear you tossing and turning at night, when you get up for a drink, when you watch

107

TV. I hear everything, and you've been doing this for a week now."

I shrugged. So, I hadn't slept in a week. Big deal. I'd sleep when I was ready.

"You see it, don't you?"

"Hmm?" I tried to sound vague as I opened the fridge for the milk, act like I didn't know what he was talking about, when in reality I did, and he was right.

"The fire. Audrey. Hear the screams." His voice was quiet, distant, thick with emotion. He saw it too.

"Yeah." I cursed and punched the fridge. "Every time I close my damn eyes. I can't sleep. I don't want to. I always end up back in that house."

"I get it. I do. You need to talk to someone, though."

"I'm seeing a therapist. Not allowed back at work until she deems me fit for duty."

"Good."

"Seen her twice already. And it's just making it worse."

"Keep going. You're not going to be fit for duty until you get some sleep."

Brody folded his arms and looked at me curiously as I finished making my coffee. I wondered how he seemed so calm and mostly unaffected by the whole thing. He was sleeping, eating, drinking like normal. I was living on coffee and sugar to keep myself from crashing.

"I'm going to see her today," he said softly. "I need to."

"Who?"

He hesitated. "Audrey."

My eyes widened, and I stared at him. He wasn't serious. "Why?"

"I need to see for myself that she'll be okay." He paused and gauged my reaction. "You should come with me. It might help."

"No." I slammed my coffee cup down on the bench, pulling my hand away when the hot liquid splashed over my skin. I was fine. I didn't need to see her.

I ran the cold water over the burning. Nothing compared to what Audrey was feeling. The pain. The helplessness. I couldn't see her. I couldn't walk into that hospital room and see her bandaged from head to toe, unable to move, unable to speak from the pain. I couldn't do it.

"If I had just got there sooner, she might have been okay." I didn't even realise I'd said the words until Brody clapped his hand on my shoulder.

"Don't do this. You can't blame yourself. There's nothing you could have done. If someone had called it in earlier, you might have got there sooner. If the air conditioner didn't have a fault, it never would have happened. You didn't do this."

He was right. Rationally, I knew he was. It wasn't my fault. I did everything I could, but it wasn't enough. No one could have predicted a fire would break out. But it didn't change the fact that there was a young girl lying in a hospital bed, with third degree burns to sixty percent of her body, who'd just lost her entire family in an instant. I couldn't imagine going through something like that. I didn't want to.

My thoughts drifted to Harper. Again. Like they had multiple times a day since I saw her last week. Harper had had a tough upbringing. Her family life was a nightmare, but she survived. She was strong. Independent. Happy...enough. She didn't let what her parents did, what happened to her brother, destroy her. It didn't send her spiralling out of control. She made something of her life.

And maybe Audrey would too.

"Okay. I'll come," I told Brody before I'd even really made up my mind to go with him. Just once. Just to convince myself that if nothing else good came of that day, at least we saved one girl.

***

I hated the smell of hospitals. They reeked of sickness and death. And the sterile white...everything did nothing to make it better. I followed Brody down the hall. Monitors beeped in every room we passed. Nurses rushed from one place to another as Brody came to a stop outside a closed door.

My steps slowed, gradually pulling farther and farther from Brody, until he turned around and noticed I wasn't behind him any longer, that I was leaning against the wall, staring at the ceiling. The two-and-a-half-hour drive to the city hadn't prepared me enough to see her. Not yet.

"Want me to go in first?" he asked. Geez, I felt like such a wimp. *Man up, Nate, and get in there. It can't be that bad.*

"Nah, I'll go."

Taking a deep breath, I followed Brody into the room and stopped at the edge of the bed. The first thing I noticed wasn't the girl completely covered in bandages. It wasn't the machines, or the tubes attached to her. It was the emptiness of the room. No flowers. No teddy bears. No balloons. Not even a single get well card.

I rubbed a hand over my chest to ease the ache that occurred the moment I realised this girl truly had no one. Where was her family? The aunts and uncles? Grandparents? Cousins? Her friends? Why hadn't anyone been to visit? Not even a god damn neighbour? No…but they were all out on the street watching as the house burnt down around her.

Brody was silent as he pulled up a chair and sat beside the bed. His head in his hands, he whispered, "I feel helpless."

I nodded. There were no words for this situation. This girl was all alone. She had nothing.

"I'll be back," I said, taking a step back and almost tripping on my own feet.

"Where—" I was out of there and running down the hall before Brody could finish asking his question.

I wasn't losing the plot. I wasn't running from the room, or my fear, or my guilt. I was on a mission. I needed to do something for this girl. For Audrey. I needed to show her it would be okay, and she wouldn't be alone.

I followed the blue signs on the walls until I came across the gift shop. The woman behind the counter stared at me in shock when I asked for the teddy bear behind her. It was four feet tall and about two feet wide. I grabbed flowers, not knowing anything about Audrey. I just picked four bunches of the most colourful flowers in the store. Balloons, two more small teddy bears, and a pink and purple blanket—not that she needed it, but it would make the room feel less like a hospital when she woke up.

I could barely carry it all back to the room, needing to stop every so often to readjust everything in my arms so I didn't drop it.

I finally made it back to Audrey's room and nudged the door open with my foot. Brody almost fell off his chair when he saw me walk in with my arms loaded.

"What are you doing?"

"Look at this room. It's empty." I shook my head sadly and handed Brody the flowers so I could put the bears down. "I can't let her wake up alone and in pain to nothing."

Brody clenched his jaw and swallowed. If I wasn't mistaken, I'd have even said his eyes glazed over before he cleared his throat and stood. "Right. Good. I'll just go and find something to put these in."

He walked out and left me alone to stare at the girl. She was asleep. On so many medications. They didn't want her to wake, not until she started healing. I wondered what would happen when she woke. Would she remember what happened? Would she block it out like Harper had? Did she have any family anywhere? Where would she go? The thought of her having absolutely no one and getting lost in the system didn't sit well with me. It wasn't fair.

Brody returned a few minutes later with four jugs of water to put the flowers in.

"Where is everyone?" I asked him.

"What do you mean?"

"Her friends and family."

Brody tucked his hands into his pockets and dropped his head. "As far as they know, there is no one. She has no other family. They have no one to contact."

"How can that be?"

"I don't know."

We sat silently for a few minutes just watching her sleep. At least her room finally looked as though someone cared and wanted to be there for her. I'd hate for her to wake up to an empty room and realise no one had been to see her.

"Ready to go?" Brody asked.

"Yeah." It was getting to me then. I couldn't get out of there fast enough. She was consuming my thoughts, and that was the last thing I needed, since she already plagued my dreams so much I couldn't sleep.

We didn't speak much on the way home. The weight of what we'd seen settled on our shoulders.

"We have to help her," Brody said.

"How?"

"I don't know, but like you said, the thought of the girl waking up alone and scared and in pain isn't right...I'm going back. I'll keep visiting her and try to find out whatever I can about her situation, see if there's anything we could do." He nodded as though he was talking himself into it.

I wasn't sure I could handle seeing her all the

time. The guilt would gnaw away at me and destroy me.

"Hungry?"

I shook my head, the same time my stomach rumbled.

"I'll take that as a yes." He laughed, and against my weak protests, pulled into the roadhouse. The last place I wanted to visit.

It was late. We'd been gone most of the afternoon, and the sun had well and truly set. I hesitated, not wanting to get out of the car in case I saw Harper. The chances were pretty high. It wasn't that I didn't want to see her. I did. I just didn't want to see her around Brody. Things were awkward enough as it was after last week.

"Dude?" Brody called to me when I sat frozen in the front seat.

Rolling my eyes, I got out and followed him inside the empty diner. Julie was behind the counter like always.

"You boys take a seat. Food won't be long."

"Thanks, Julie," I said and wandered over to a booth. It was pretty bad that we didn't even have to order anymore. We walked in, and she fed us.

"How'd you go with the ice machine?" Brody asked, spinning the salt shaker on the table.

"What?" I frowned in confusion.

"Julie wanted you to look at the ice machine last week."

"Oh, yeah…" I snapped my fingers and pointed at him. "That's right. Uh, nothing. False alarm. It was fine."

Brody narrowed his eyes at me. I thought it was

a good lie.

"What?"

"Nothing." He smiled up at Julie when she delivered our food.

Halfway through eating, Brody's phone rang.

"Damn. I gotta get this...Hello? Yeah. Really?" He listened as the caller spoke. "Okay. No, that's great." Another pause. "Yeah, I'll bring her down. Thanks, man." He hung up and wiped his mouth clean before standing up.

I raised my eyebrows in question. Where was he going halfway through a meal?

"I, ah, gotta go. That was a buddy of mine at the police station."

"The police station?"

"I had him check into Chace after he showed up at the uni last week to harass Kenzie, and he's got some info. I'm going to take her in to chat with him."

"Okay, sure." I took a sip of my chocolate milkshake that only Julie knew how to make.

"You coming?"

I went to stand but thought better of it. "No. I'm still eating."

"You right for a lift home?"

"Yeah, I'll be fine. I'll call Linc."

"All right," he said and walked off.

I finished my meal and leaned my head against the back of the booth.

"You look like shit." I peeled my eyes open to see Johnny standing above me with the elastic from his hairnet cutting into one eye.

"Thanks," I grumbled and yawned. And before I

could stop myself, I asked, "Harper upstairs?"

"Depends."

"On what?"

"Whether you're going to go up there only to tell her you can't be friends or something stupid like that again."

"No. I..." I couldn't argue with him or tell him I'd never do that, because I basically told her that last week, that we needed to keep our distance. But right then, I really needed a friend, and not just any friend. I needed Harper.

"You've been warned." He pulled his spatula out from nowhere and put it against my neck like a knife.

"Got it." I raised my hands in surrender.

Johnny grunted and walked off, so I dragged my feet to the stairs that led to Harper's room.

CHAPTER TWELVE

Harper

The words were blurring together. Stretched out on my stomach on my bed, I'd been reading this stupid text for so long, I was sure my eyes would be permanently crossed. Earphones in my ears, my entire playlist had repeated twice. It was almost the end of the semester, and I had an exam on Friday to study for. I didn't understand why our uni ran on a different schedule to most that had already finished for the year, but it did. Country towns, I guessed. I was looking forward to the break.

A song I really enjoyed came on, and once again I began tapping my highlighter on my book while simultaneously kicking my feet and nodding to the beat. Multitasking at its finest.

Something brushed against my ankle and jerked my foot. Must have been a blanket or something. Then it happened again, only it wasn't brushing. It was grabbing. Wrapping its warm fingers around my leg. I froze. Someone was in my room and

117

touching me.

Heart pounding in my chest, and my breaths coming hard and fast, I yanked the earphones out of my ears and twisted to look.

Nate.

I breathed out a sigh and slumped back onto the mattress.

"Sorry." He shifted my feet and sat on the edge of my bed. "I knocked, but you didn't hear."

"Music." I held up my headphones in response.

His warm hands lifted my legs and placed them in his lap. He didn't bat an eye at the fact I was only wearing a tank top and underwear.

"What are you doing here?" I asked after a while of silence. He looked broken. His normally styled hair was a mess. His eyes had lost their sparkle. They were red and puffy and had bigger black bags beneath them than I had in my closet.

His fingers began kneading the muscles in my calves, starting just above my Achilles and inching slowly up my leg. I bit my lip to stop from moaning. I'd never had a leg massage before, and it was amazing.

"I could do with a friend."

"And everyone else is busy?" I couldn't stop the bitterness in my voice even though his hands on my skin were making me feel everything but bitter.

"No. I don't know. I didn't try them. I wanted to see you."

"Why?"

He didn't answer. He concentrated on the movements of his hands, the pressure he applied.

"I haven't slept," he murmured.

"Since when?"

"The fire."

"Nate…"

"I know. I just can't sleep. Every time I close my eyes, I'm back there."

I pushed myself to a sitting position and picked up all my books, papers, pens, and highlighters and dumped them on the floor.

"You can't go on not sleeping. Come here." I grabbed his hands and pulled him toward me.

He let me, climbing onto the bed beside me. "I shouldn't stay long, you know…" he said as he settled his head into my pillow.

All resentment I'd been feeling for the past week gone. It didn't matter that he made me share my darkest secret. It didn't matter that he told me we were only friends. It didn't matter that he hadn't bothered to visit or talk to me, his friend, for the last week. All that mattered was that he was here, and he needed me. He wanted to see me.

"You should…stay. Just to sleep."

"I can't sleep. I don't want to."

"With me. I'll be right here. You're going to hurt yourself if you don't get some rest soon."

"Harper."

"I'm not taking no for answer." I sat up and crawled to the end of the bed to remove his shoes. Pointing my finger toward the roof I said, "Up."

Nate sat, so I removed his shirt and threw it on the chair in the corner of my room. Then I thought better of it and grabbed it for myself instead.

Nate groaned.

"What?" I turned to face him after I'd pulled his

119

shirt on and removed my tank from underneath.

"You in my shirt." He flopped back onto the pillow and covered his face with his hands.

"You don't want me to wear it?" I looked down and fiddled with the hem.

"No. I mean..." He dragged his hands over his face and lifted them behind his head before nailing me with a gaze that made my knees tremble. "I just like you in it too much."

"Well, that's perfect," I said, moving to lie beside him.

"Why?"

"Because I like wearing them." I lifted my head when he shifted his arm to wrap it around me and rested it on his chest. Friends didn't lie together like this. "And I like you better out of them." I placed my hand on his chest and tapped my fingers in time with his heartbeat.

He cursed. "You can't say that sort of thing, friend."

We weren't friends. When was he going to give up the charade? We couldn't stay away from each other. We'd proven that time and time again. A three-month-long secret affair followed by a three-month-long break from spending time together in any way. And it all came undone when Indie returned, forcing us back together. The pull was so much stronger this time. It was undeniable. Tangible. Strong. There was no fighting it.

His lips pressed against the top of my head, and his fingers found their way under his shirt to trace small circles on my hip bone, searing my skin with his touch. Friends definitely didn't lie together like this.

I fell asleep with my hand on his heart and his lips in my hair. But that wasn't the best part. The best part was he fell asleep too.

Sometime through the night he became restless, tossed and turned. Shook his head and muttered incoherently while still asleep. The moonlight cast shadows on his face, outlining the pained expression, and I knew he was having a bad dream. Not wanting to wake him because he was finally sleeping, and he needed it more than anything else, I whispered, "It's okay. It's just a dream," over and over while gently smoothing the creases on his forehead. He calmed down after a while, and I was able to drift back to sleep.

I woke in the morning to find myself completely tangled with Nate. Our bare legs were woven together, and I was practically lying on top of him. My arms were wrapped around his waist, my chest pressed to his, and his hands…

His hands.

I felt them everywhere.

My skin tingled from his touch. One hand twisted firmly into my hair, cradling the back of my head and holding me against him while the other dragged leisurely circles under my shirt…his shirt. Up and down my back, over my hips, down my thighs, up my inner thighs, dangerously close to the territory friends did not enter, across my stomach, and around my ribs.

He was awake.

I twisted my neck to look at him and was met by his dark blue eyes shining back at me. The bags under his eyes had faded, the redness almost gone.

"Good morning." I bit my lip to hide my smile. His hair was a mess, worse than it was last night, but he had some colour back in his cheeks and didn't appear as drained.

"Hi, friend." He gave me a lazy half smile.

"Still going with that name, are you?"

"Of course. We're friends." He wiggled beneath me and closed his eyes. Getting comfortable again, he adjusted his hold on me so both hands were clasped behind my back.

"Friends don't get this close."

"Friends who snuggle do. We're friends who snuggle." His voice was tired and thick with sleep, so I didn't say anything else. He needed to rest.

We didn't snuggle. It was so much more than snuggling.

As much as I didn't want to move, I had a lot of studying to do. So, once Nate had fallen asleep again, I reluctantly unwrapped my body from his and moved to the floor. I immediately missed the warmth of his skin against mine. Sticking the tip of my pen in my mouth, I chewed on it as I contemplated getting back in bed and "snuggling," as Nate put it.

Common sense prevailed, and I turned away from the bed and attempted to concentrate on what I was reading. But it was useless. I couldn't stop myself from sneaking glances at Nate every few seconds. He was beautiful when he slept. So peaceful. Innocent. Not a worry in the world. It was when he woke up fully that I feared. I just hoped the night's sleep he had was enough to get him back to normal.

My bedroom door opened, and I whipped my head around to see who it was. Uncle Johnny and Aunt Julie always knocked, so I knew it wouldn't be them.

"Hey," Kenzie greeted when she stepped into the room before stopping short, her mouth hanging open and her eyes wide.

"It's not what it looks like." I raised my hands in defence.

"It looks like Nate is sleeping half naked in your bed." She crept over to the bed and tilted her head as she inspected him.

"Okay. It is what it looks like. Sort of. He's sleeping. Nothing else. That's all that happened." I didn't know why I was explaining myself to her. Maybe because she'd likely ask a trillion questions later. But I knew why I lied.

I couldn't tell her that sometime through the night, I woke up to find Nate's hand under my shirt, cupping my breast. And I couldn't tell her that his hand drifted south. Just like I couldn't tell her that he removed my underwear and his boxer shorts. I also couldn't tell her that he set every nerve ending in my body alight with only a few touches, a few kisses, and a few strokes of his…

"How could you let nothing happen? Have you had a look at this man?" She waved her hands over his body and interrupted my memories of the night before.

Nate groaned and rolled onto his back.

"For the love of…look at that," she huffed and pointed to his…hips? Abs? Crotch? I wasn't sure.

123

"How could you pass up an opportunity to lick that body?"

"Will you keep your voice down?" I tried to shush her and purposely ignored her previous question. Because I didn't pass up any opportunity to lick that body. My lips were rather well acquainted with the fine specimen that was Nate. "He's sleeping."

"I can see that." She stretched out her fingers and lowered them toward Nate.

"What are you doing? Stop." I grabbed her hand and pulled it back before she could touch him.

"I just want to feel. See if it's as hard as it looks." She winked and yanked her hand out of mine, slowly lowering it until she hovered just over his shorts.

"You are not going to feel him up."

"Oh, come on! Get your mind out of the gutter, Harper. I just want to see if…" She moved her hand again and touched his…hair? "If his hair is set rock hard like it always looks, or if he uses a soft product. I need something soft to tame all my curls."

I hadn't realised I'd been clenching my jaw until that moment when I suddenly relaxed because I knew Kenzie wasn't going to touch Nate inappropriately. I quickly pulled on a pair of jeans and dragged her from the room.

"What are you doing here, Kenz?"

"The question is, why is Nate asleep in your bed if nothing is going on?" I followed her downstairs to grab some food.

"He's just…he was tired. He's been having

trouble sleeping since the fire, and he came in here last night. You should have seen him. He looked dead on his feet. I made him lie down and go to sleep, and he hasn't moved since last night."

"Yeah, I heard. Brody told me."

"Oh, you are Brody are such good friends now, huh?"

"Uh-huh. And you're wearing Nate's shirt because…?"

"Because I like it," I said, and Kenzie nodded.

"Because you like him," she said.

I nodded once then realised what I was doing. "What? No." I shook my head furiously to get my point across. "I like him as a friend. That's it. We're just friends."

If that wasn't the biggest lie I'd ever told, I didn't know what was.

"I don't believe you, but I'm going to let it slide because I have news. Sort of."

We sat at the counter with our food. It was well past lunchtime now.

"What?"

"Brody's friend dug up some stuff on Chace, and I don't know what to do about it."

"Like what?"

"Like pretty bad stuff. Like assault. Attempted sexual assault. It was only stopped because Ryder beat him within an inch of his life," she said before taking a huge bite of her burger.

"You're kidding?"

"Nope."

"Who did he assault? It wasn't Bailey, was it?"

Kenzie's eyes narrowed. "I don't know. I don't

125

think so. Ryder would have told me if it was. Brody's friend didn't give too much information, just enough to make me wary. So now, do I mention it to Chace so he knows I know what an asshole he is? Or do I take it to the lawyers and fight for custody of Cole?"

I wasn't entirely convinced Ryder would tell her if it was Bailey. He didn't tell her he was arrested for assaulting Chace, and he didn't tell her Johnny bailed him out

"Both. I think it'll be the only way stop him from harassing you any further."

"Maybe. It's all so messed up. Why can't things ever be simple?"

"Life isn't simple."

CHAPTER THIRTEEN

Nate

It was boys' night, apparently, or so Jack insisted when he got to town that morning. But I had no desire to go out or be social. My much-needed sleep had been short-lived. I'd not slept again for the last two nights, and I blamed therapy.

I swore my therapist was a masochist. She seemed to enjoy making me suffer, making me relive the incident over and over again. Like it was going to make it any better. Surely, moving on and trying not to think about it would be better than going through and analysing every last detail and thought or emotion that occurred as a result of the fire. But no, she liked to get me worked up and frustrated, only to tell me our time was up for the day.

I stormed out of the therapist's office and got in my car, in desperate need of a drink. Maybe a boys' night wouldn't be so bad. We were meeting at the one place I failed to avoid no matter how much I

127

tried. The roadhouse. Jack wanted to try the best burgers in the state, so I raced home to have a shower and get changed. Our options for a night out were pretty limited in a town this small. There was only one bar, and it was a dive. But it had cold beer and a pool table, so that was where we were headed after dinner.

I walked into the diner at the roadhouse an hour later and waved at Julie. The guys were in the booth already. It seemed as if that one particular booth was reserved for us, even though I'd never seen anyone else in the diner.

"Nate," Jack said and held out his hand for a fist bump when I sat down.

"Hey. Good to see you, man."

"Wish I could say the same." Jack frowned and pinched my cheeks. He tilted my head back then pulled it down before turning it from side to side. What was he doing? This guy had no boundaries and no clue about personal space. I slapped his hands away, and he simply laughed. "You know, bloodshot eyes and pasty skin aren't a good look on you."

"Whatever." I knew I looked like shit. I wasn't sleeping, but I couldn't do anything about it. Sleeping tablets weren't even working. Nothing worked, except for those few peaceful hours in Harper's bed. I just figured I'd crash eventually.

My thoughts drifted back to Harper. We gave in again. I didn't mean for it to happen. I didn't mean to fall asleep in her bed. I didn't mean to lose myself in her. But I did, and I wanted to again, even though we swore no more. It couldn't happen again.

Brody was my cousin, and it would kill him to find out.

"So, this is Blackhill." Jack looked around the diner as though Blackhill was only the roadhouse, his nose screwed up in disgust. "Why does everyone like it so much?"

"It's home," Ryder said.

"It's not so bad. The beach is pretty good," Linc said.

"Oh, can we go surfing while I'm here?"

"No."

"Why not?"

"You're the most uncoordinated person I've ever seen. You want to surf, Ace can teach."

"Ace." Jack sniggered as though he knew the meaning behind the nickname.

"Shut up." Linc balled up a napkin and threw it at him.

"Aww…I've missed you so much, Lincoln."

Ryder laughed, and Linc sighed. "Why did we invite you, again?"

"Because I'm Jack."

"Jack-ass." Linc grinned, causing Ryder to cough on air.

"I resent that. It hurts, right here." Jack beat his fist on his chest, his smile dropping from his face and his eyes glazing over. Hell. He looked like he was going to cry.

"It does not." Ryder rolled his eyes.

"You're right, but I totally had you there, didn't I?" He tipped his head back and let out a laugh.

The kitchen doors swung open, and Harper walked out carrying a tray of burgers and fries. My jaw dropped. She looked hot. Hotter than normal. Something about her in biker boots and skin-tight black leather pants. They looked painted on, and I had the sudden urge to peel them from her long legs. Linc kicked me under the table and shook his head once. She approached the table and gave me a small smile before saying hi to everyone else. I snapped my jaw shut and sat a little straighter.

"Harper?" Jack's eyes widened, and his lips pulled up into a smile. He shoved me sideways, forcing me out of the booth so he could greet Harper properly.

"Hi, Jack." She pulled a face that was equal parts confused and amused when he wrapped her in his arms and spun her around.

"It's so good to see you."

"Ooh, you're a friendly one, aren't you?" She laughed when he kissed her cheek. My stomach churned, and my chest tightened. She never laughed like that when she was with me.

"Too friendly," Linc seethed.

"Hey, I told you I missed Indie. And it's not my fault she's, like, the best kisser in the world," he teased.

"What?" I gaped at him before flicking my gaze to Linc, whose jaw was set, his lips pressed in a firm line. "You kissed my sister?"

"Oh, wait." Jack folded an arm across his chest and tapped his chin with the other hand while looking at the ceiling in thought. "It's totally my fault she's a good kisser. Taught her everything I know," he said with a squeal of delight that soon turned into fits of laughter.

Ryder banged his head against the table while Linc groaned and gripped a knife in his hand.

"And to answer your question, Nathaniel, yes, I totally kissed your sister. Multiple times. Remember? Fiji? The plan?" he asked.

How could I forget? He acted like a total dick, treated Indie like a piece of meat, kissed her every chance he got in the hopes Linc would finally man up and stake his claim...or whatever. It worked.

He looked at Linc. "You're still welcome. Even though you never thanked me."

"You don't deserve a thank you. And you kissed my damn fiancée this morning. In. Front. Of. Me."

Harper gasped and stared at them both with wide eyes.

"Would you rather I do it behind your back? 'Cause I'm good with that."

Shit.

Jack was a dead man.

"Jack. Enough."

"Okay, sorry. I'll keep my lips," he paused and took in the expression on Linc's face, "and tongue to myself. Happy?" He pouted.

"No."

"You love me." He flopped back into the booth and smiled innocently at Linc.

"Not likely."

"But your fiancée does." He rested his head in his hands and pursed his lips, making kissing noises.

Harper giggled beside me.

"I give up." Ryder threw his hands in the air and leaned back against the seat. "I'm not saving your

131

ass this time."

"Ahh," Jack sighed in contentment. "It's so good to see you guys."

"Wish I could say the same," Linc muttered under his breath. Linc had nothing to worry about, and he knew it. Aside from the fact that Indie was head over heels in love with Linc, Jack was gay and not interested in Indie that way. He was just good, too good at acting and knew how to press Linc's buttons. Indie and Jack were best friends.

"Get used to me, Linc baby! I'm all yours. All summer." Linc's fist tightened on the knife. "Hey, where's Brody? I thought he'd be here."

"Nightshift," I said.

"Oh, shoot." Harper looked at her watch. "I gotta go or they'll be ringing to see where I am. You guys have a good night. Jack, try not to get dead." She waved goodbye and left.

My eyes trained on her ass the whole way to the door.

"Playing with fire, man," Linc said.

I shrugged. It was nothing. I was totally in control. Nothing was going on. We were friends.

"Huh?" Jack asked, and Ryder looked between Linc and me, lips pinched between his fingers. The guy noticed everything.

"Nothing." I reached for a burger. "Let's eat so we can get out of here."

"Oh, my god. This burger is so good," Jack mumbled through a mouthful of food.

"Don't let Johnny hear you say that. He'll come to brag," Ryder said.

After we finished eating and insisting on paying

the full bill, because Julie never charged us when we came in, and I was concerned how they still managed to run a business with no customers and no profit, we made our way into the centre of town to the little bar.

"Wow. Blackhill has a bookstore?" Jack asked incredulously. "I'll have to check it out while I'm here."

"It's a great bookstore," Ryder said before adding vaguely, "Lots of good memories."

I laughed. "Good memories of a bookstore? Man, you gotta get out more."

"Trust me." He smiled wistfully, and I figured it had something to do with Bailey. I was pretty sure she worked in a bookstore when they were in high school. I remembered Indie saying she was hanging out there and thought it was weird. Indie never read, and she only went because Bailey was there.

We approached the bar and could hear the music echoing down the street.

"One bar in town?" Jack asked.

"Yep."

"Hmmm."

"Don't like it? You can always go home," Linc suggested.

"I'm sure I'll love it. You're not getting rid of me that easy."

We found a table in the back corner, and Ryder went to get a couple of jugs of beer. The bar was relatively quiet. The town was small, so the number of young people who ventured out at night was low. Most places were guaranteed to be quiet. Traffic was almost non-existent. There was no noise. It was peaceful. I liked it.

After a couple of beers, Jack and Ryder got up to play pool, and Linc went to get more drinks for the table. I didn't want to move. My body ached from exhaustion. My phone buzzed in my pocket, and I pulled it out to see a text.

Harper: Hi, friend.

I smiled. I couldn't help it. My thoughts drifted back to her and her leather pants that I wanted to run my hands all over. I was screwed.

Nate: That's my line.

Harper: I learned from the best. How are you?

Nate: Exhausted.

Harper: Have you slept?

Nate: Not since your bed.

Harper: That's not good. I'm worried. What are you doing tonight?

Nate: Watching Jack and Ryder play pool and drinking beer.

Nate: What are you girls doing?

Harper: Pillow fights in our underwear. You know? The usual girls' night shenanigans.

We're going to paint our nails and braid our hair later too ;)

I barked out a laugh and thought about my response.

"What's so funny?" Linc asked when he returned with another jug of beer.

"Nothing."

Nate: I'd like to see that, friend.

I waited for a response. The dots moving at the bottom of the screen indicated Harper was typing and deleting the message and retyping.

"Who are you texting?"

"Harper."

"Nate." His voice held a hint of warning. It wasn't that he didn't approve. He liked Harper. It was just that he didn't want to see Brody get hurt either.

"What? We're friends. That's it," I said, bringing my glass to my lips.

"Friends who snuggle?" Linc asked, with an eyebrow raised and an amused expression on his face. I just about choked on my beer. Snuggle? I'd said that exact thing to Harper after waking up in her bed.

"What?"

"Friends don't snuggle like that."

"How do you even know?" I glanced at my phone again. Still no response. Did I push it too far?

"Come on. Kenzie walked in on you in her bed. She told Bailey. Bailey told Indie, and Indie told me. Secrets don't stay quiet for long."

I took a drink of my beer, the cool, bitter liquid soothing my suddenly dry throat. "It's not like that."

Linc folded his hands on the table and waited.

I checked my phone again.

"Friends also don't obsessively check for text messages."

"I fell asleep. Passed out from exhaustion." It was the truth. I just left out the rest of the night.

"So, you're sleeping better now?"

"Not at all. Haven't slept since that night at Harper's. The nightmares are getting worse." I drained my beer and poured another one. Maybe I could drink myself to sleep.

"Hmm…" Linc stood and rapped his fist on the table. "Just be careful. Play with fire, and someone's bound to get burned. You've got a message," he said and walked over to Ryder and Jack.

I looked down at my phone and saw a message from Harper.

Opening the message, I spat my beer out, spraying it everywhere.

Harper: This what you were imagining?

I stared at the photo she sent. I couldn't believe she actually took the photo, let alone sent it to me. Her hair was twisted into two small schoolgirl type braids on the sides of her head, and she posed in front of a bathroom mirror in nothing but her underwear and a pillow placed strategically in front of her body to hide everything. But I could clearly see a hint of skin on her lower back where she arched, pushing her chest forward, her bare shoulder blade, the curve of her hip covered by nothing but small scrap of black material. Her left foot was lifted behind her, and she balanced on her right. Her lips pursed as though blowing a kiss at the phone she held in her right hand and aimed at the mirror.

As though blowing a kiss to me.

Shit.

Nate: Are you trying to get me killed?

Harper: You said you wanted to see...

Nate: I thought you were joking. No one actually has pillow fights in their underwear.

Harper: I was joking. We're watching a movie and drinking a bottle of wine.

That meant she purposely stripped out of her clothes and posed with a pillow. For me.

Nate: You can't send me something like that and not expect me to have inappropriate thoughts.

Harper: Oh, do tell, friend...I'm listening. What are these inappropriate thoughts of yours? ;)

I groaned and dropped my head into my hands.

What was I doing? I wasn't seriously entertaining this idea. But I was. I lost it the moment she cried in my lap over her brother and traumatic past. I was beyond the point of no return when I fell asleep with her in my arms, because as exhausted as I was, I was sure I only slept because she was there. She was the calm in the storm.

Nate: *I'm thinking how much I want to lick the two dimples on your lower back.*

Harper: *Nate...*

I hesitated, thinking about what I wanted to do, about the right thing to do, what I should do, and what I wanted to do.

Jack came over to the table in a rush. "We have to go," he said urgently. I looked up to see Linc and Ryder behind him, frowning in confusion.

"Okay," I agreed, not really caring what was so urgent that we had leave right then. All I cared about was finishing things with Harper.

Then I typed the only thing I could in a message to Harper.

CHAPTER FOURTEEN

Harper

"Who are you texting?" Kenzie asked, pulling my attention from my phone held firmly in my grasp. What was taking him so long to respond? Maybe I pushed things too far when I sent the photo. He was adamant that we were just friends, but that wasn't good enough for me anymore.

"Just a friend," I said, knowing she'd put two and two together.

"You don't have friends." Indie laughed into her wineglass.

"I do so. Why does everyone keep saying that?"

"Because you only hang out with us."

It was true. They were my only friends, and now I was trying to talk Nate back into my bed after I ended things in the first place. He was Indie's brother. He was Brody's cousin. How messed up was that?

Maybe I should text him and tell him…what? That I'd only been messing around. That I didn't want him as anything more than a friend. But I couldn't do that. Not now, not after another "one night" together. I'd be lying to him, to myself, and to my heart.

"How's the Chace situation?" I asked Kenzie, changing the subject.

"Haven't seen or heard from him since he showed up at school, so I don't know. It's a good thing, I guess."

"Maybe not." Indie frowned at her phone.

"What?"

"Linc just texted me to say they were leaving the bar early because Chace showed up."

Kenzie winced and closed her eyes.

"Ryder?" Bailey asked, concern etching her features.

"Didn't see him." Indie nodded in confirmation. "They got him out of there before he ran into Chace."

"Thank god." Kenzie sighed. "He can't get into any more trouble."

My phone buzzed in my hands.

Nate: Screw the consequences.

My fingers loosened their grip on the phone, letting it fall to the floor.

All eyes turned to me.

"Sorry."

I picked up my phone and typed a reply.

Harper: Nate...

Nate: Brody is working all night. I'm going home now. It's your decision, friend.

And he was still calling me "friend." What did I do? Should I meet him, or stay here with my friends? He was giving me what I wanted, and I was suddenly unsure what to do. We agreed after the other night it could never happen again. It was a one-time thing. A one-time thing that still had my body tingling. A one-time thing that consumed my thoughts. Seriously, I was like a teenage boy thinking about sex with how often my thoughts wafted over to a naked Nate.

"You look like you've seen a ghost," Bailey said.

"I, uh…I have to go." I guessed I'd made up my mind.

"Harper," Kenzie warned.

"I have to, Kenzie. I can't…," I paused, trying to think of the right words. "It's just something I have to do, okay?"

She held up her hands in surrender. "Just be careful."

"Always."

I said goodbye, grabbed my bag, and left. Bailey and Ryder's place wasn't that far from Nate's small apartment, so I could walk there easily enough. I just hoped I didn't stumble across any of the others on my way. That would be too many questions I couldn't answer.

***

One look at Nate as he walked toward the stairs,

I knew I had made the right decision. If not for the reasons I was expecting, but for the one that was glaringly obvious.

"Hi, friend." He smiled when he saw me waiting for him, but it didn't reach his eyes. They were drawn and red. He was exhausted.

"Hi." I stood and let him link his fingers with mine, pulling me up the stairs to his apartment door. He never let go, not until we were in his room, standing quietly face to face.

"You came," he whispered, his free hand reaching for my hip. He tugged me to him and dropped his head to my shoulder. "I wasn't sure you would."

"Screw the consequences, right?"

He dropped my hand and reached for the hem of my shirt, lifting it over my head and dropping it on the floor.

"Screw them. Screw everything." He pulled back to look at me, his fingers dancing along my collarbone before they dragged down over my arms and back to my hips, and then he dropped to his knees in front of me. He leisurely trailed his hands down my legs until he reached my boots. He lifted one leg and placed it on his lap so he could release the zipper and remove my shoe before repeating the process with the other one.

Still kneeling, Nate looked up at me, a dazed expression on his face as he caught my gaze. My hands were in his hair, my fingers aching to touch him in any way. I was lost in his eyes, lost in the moment. I couldn't speak. Couldn't form a thought as his hands rubbed circles on my legs, inching higher and higher until he popped the button on my waistband and slid my leather pants down my legs and discarded them with my shirt.

With a kiss to the top of my thigh that sent chills up my spine, he stood, removed his shirt, and handed it to me. I took it from him, clutching it in my fingers as I stood frozen to the spot, watching him kick off his shoes and drop his jeans to the floor with mine. He took his shirt from my hands and pulled it over my head because I couldn't function.

What was wrong with me?

Nate wrapped his arms around my waist and pulled me to him, my hands finding their way around the back of his neck and into his hair once again. He gripped my thighs and lifted me, forcing my legs around his waist while he buried his face in the crook of my neck. It seemed to be his favourite spot.

"You smell so good," he said, inhaling the scent of my skin, my hair, my body wash. "Sweet…like honey."

Carrying me over to his bed, he laid me down gently and climbed in beside me. We were on our sides facing each other. Our fingers twisted together beneath the covers, our eyes locked in their own embrace.

"Nate, you need to sleep." He couldn't keep going the way he was. It was going to kill him.

"I don't want to." He folded one arm under his head and watched me.

"It's not good for you."

"You're good for me."

I smiled. "For now. This is all going to blow up when people find out."

"When Brody finds out, you mean?"

I nodded. "We agreed it was a one-time thing."

He laughed. "Yeah, we said that in Fiji too. That worked out well."

"One night, Nate. That was all it was meant to be." As much as I wanted this.

"Screw the consequences. Remember? One night isn't enough. One night in Fiji clearly wasn't enough if the three months that followed were anything to go by. And all that one night this week did was serve to remind me how good we are together. Naked, of course. I'm done fighting this." His squeezed my hand. His eyelids fluttered closed before he snapped them open again. "I want a hundred 'one nights.'" His voice trailed away as sleep finally overtook him.

"Screw the consequences another day," I whispered, watching his breaths even out as he fell into a deep sleep. I wanted a hundred nights too. Only I feared that still wouldn't be enough.

I rolled onto my side, pressing my back against his chest, and wrapped his arm around my waist, falling into peaceful sleep with him.

I fully intended on waking early and leaving before Brody got home from his shift, but that didn't happen if the sound of the front door closing was anything to go by. Nate woke with a jolt beside me, almost jumping out of the bed.

"What was that?" He looked around frantically.

"Shh, it's okay. It's just Brody getting home," I reassured him.

"Okay." He nodded, still half asleep, and pulled me into his arms as he settled back into his pillows.

Then he froze.

"Brody's home?"

I nodded, not wanting to speak in case Brody heard. Linc had told me once the walls were thin.

"Dammit. We have to sneak you out of here."

"Thanks. That makes me feel real good about myself." I shoved him away.

"Sorry. That sounded worse than I thought. But you know…" He threw his hands in the air to emphasise the urgency of the situation.

"I know."

What if he came looking for Nate? What if he walked into Nate's room?

"I should get dressed." I rolled over and kicked my legs out of the bed, but Nate's arm around my waist pulled me back.

"Not yet. We have at least an hour of him wasting time before he has a shower and goes to bed. Stay a little longer."

I smiled at him and leaned in, resting my head on his chest. Not much I could do until Brody went to sleep, so I might as well enjoy the moment while it lasted.

We fell asleep. Again.

"Dammit. Nate." I shook him gently, not wanting to wake him, but needing to get the hell out of there. I had an exam in the afternoon.

"Hmmm."

"The shower is running. I need to go." I climbed out of the bed and pulled on my clothes, deciding to carry my shoes so they didn't echo down the hall.

"Nate."

"Coming." He groaned as he sat up and stretched his neck.

Padding to the door, he opened it just enough to put his head through.

"Coast is clear," he whispered, looking at me over his shoulder. I followed him on tippy-toes through the apartment to the front door, careful not to make a noise.

"Thanks for having a sleepover, friend," Nate said softly as he opened the door to let me out. I stood on the threshold and slid my boots on carefully.

"Anytime."

"Who's at the door?" Brody's voiced sounded from behind Nate. My eyes widened, and I took a step back. Nate turned on his heels and faced Brody, attempting to close the door in my face. I rolled my eyes.

"Uh…"

Brody looked over Nate's shoulder. "Harper, hey." He smiled, his eyes lighting up. Nate dropped his head briefly before stepping to the side and opening the door wider.

Brody stood beside Nate, in a towel. Water still dripped down his chest.

"What are you doing here?"

"I—I, umm…" I panicked. What could my excuse be? I glanced around and noticed Nate's jacket thrown over the side of the sofa. "I was returning Nate's jacket."

I mentally patted myself on the back. That was a valid reason, right?

"Why did you have his jacket?" Brody frowned.

I was done. I couldn't come up with another lie.

"She found me stumbling down the street last night after leaving the bar and gave me a lift home," Nate answered.

"And the chick?" Brody asked.

Nate and I looked at each other.

"What chick?"

"The one in your bed this morning."

My heart dropped. He saw? But he didn't know it was me. My shoulders sagged in relief.

"Umm." Nate scratched the back of his head.

"Told you he was shagging his way out of a broken heart," Brody said to me with a laugh.

I didn't find it funny. It only served as a reminder of everyone Nate had apparently been with since me.

"You went into my room?" Nates hands clenched.

"Only to check if you were home."

"Where else would I be at seven a.m.?" His shoulders were tense.

"Who knows? You hardly sleep. And when I didn't get home to find you drinking coffee straight from the pot, I stuck my head in to check."

"Stay out of my room."

"Whatever. Whoever she is, I'm just glad she managed to get you to fall asleep, so you don't keep me awake all night thumping around the house." Brody yawned. "Okay, I'm beat. See you, Harper."

"Yeah, bye," I said quietly as Brody walked away. I turned and walked down the stairs.

"Harper?" Nate called. "Wait."

I didn't wait. I didn't want to have the talk. The one I knew was coming. The one that said those other girls didn't mean anything. Those other girls were nothing. Whatever. I had no right to be jealous. I was the one who ended things, after all.

Nate cursed, and then his footsteps thudded down the stairs behind me. I reached the front of the apartment building and stepped outside before he caught me.

"Stop." He grabbed me and spun me around, pushing me back until the cold concrete wall was pressed into my spine.

His hands cupped my face, and he rested his forehead on mine. "Brody exaggerates."

"So, there was no one else in the last three months?" I didn't touch him, even though I craved it.

Nate shook his head. "There was one. One, and nothing happened."

"Yeah, sure. Whatever. Not like we were in a relationship then, and it's not like we're in one now."

I didn't know why I was getting so worked up.

"No. But we keep coming back to each other. There's something between us. Some sort of magnetic pull that keeps drawing us back together in one way or another. I told you last night, I was done fighting. We keep dancing around each other, and I'm tired of it," he said, and then he kissed me.

"Tired of it?"

"Exhausted," he said with a smile. "I can't stay away any longer."

He kissed the hell out of me.

148

His mouth was hot and needy on mine, his fingers firm on my neck while his thumbs grazed my cheeks. My body betrayed me and melted in his arms. I brought my hands up to his chest and clutched his shirt to pull him closer. Butterflies erupted in my stomach, and my knees gave out. Nate caught me and hoisted me up until my legs were around his waist. His teeth pulled my bottom lip into his mouth, making me gasp.

All thoughts had left my head.

All hesitation was gone.

Our tongues slid together, our hands moved everywhere.

Touching too much.

Not touching enough.

I didn't care that we were outside his apartment building, that people could see us, or at any moment Brody could come looking for him and catch us. I just needed his kisses.

Nate pulled back, his breath heavy and laboured. He released me, and I slid down the wall like the pile of mush I was.

With one light peck on the lips, he said, "We'll keep it quiet. No one needs to know. Screw the consequences. I'm in. Ball's in your court, friend."

And then he walked back inside.

CHAPTER FIFTEEN

Nate

"How are the sessions going, love?" Mum pulled up a chair beside me on the porch of Linc and Indie's shack, wineglass in her fingers.

They'd just finished the speeches and were now in full party mode.

"Waste of time," I said, nursing my now warm beer. I wasn't in the right frame of mind to celebrate, much less party. "They seem to make things worse, not better."

"You look a little better today, though. Still tired, but not as bad as the other day. Are you sleeping?"

My lips pulled into a small smile. I only slept when Harper was beside me. "It comes and goes."

I didn't sleep last night at all. Tossed and turned all night. Images of Audrey played in my mind like a movie reel. The screams of her family echoed in my head as though I had a playlist on repeat. Therapy wasn't working. Going to visit Audrey wasn't helping. I'd slept for two nights in the past week and a half, and both times were only when Harper was there.

Harper helped.

But I hadn't seen Harper since yesterday morning after almost getting caught by Brody sneaking her out. Thankfully, he was too tired to notice anything suspicious, but it was a close call. Particularly when he saw a woman in my bed. We had to be more careful.

I was watching her now, though. Down on the beach with Indie, Kenzie, and Bailey, all laughing at something. They looked so carefree and happy.

"Give the therapy sessions some time. Who knows? It might surprise you." Mum reached over and patted my knee encouragingly. "Anything else on your mind?"

I shook my head and pulled my gaze away from Harper to look at my mother.

"Really, Nate?"

I nodded. "Really." I nodded again, just for assurance.

"Hmmm." She pursed her lips and frowned, not buying the lie at all.

"I'm just getting bored. I want to get back to work. I hate sitting on my ass all day." And I did. I wasn't the type of person who could do mindless activities all day long. I enjoyed working. At least I did, before the fire.

"You don't want to rush it, though. If you go back before you're ready, you could make things worse, for yourself or your team."

"I know. It just sucks."

We were silent for a while, watching the waves

crash against the shore in the moonlight. I was focused on Harper more than anything. On the way her laugh carried in the wind. On the way her hair blew in the ocean breeze, giving me a view of her neck, the skin so pale it glowed.

"Have you seen Audrey again?" my mother asked, interrupting my thoughts.

"Yesterday." I sighed and rubbed a hand over my face.

"How is she?"

"Still bad. They expect her to wake soon. Brody wants to be there when she does. He visits her every day before his shift."

"He's a good man. So kind and caring. Would do anything to help a person out."

"He would," I agreed, and it made my stomach churn. He liked visiting Audrey. He was good at it. It didn't bother him sitting there in silence with her. He'd taken to reading gossip magazines to her and playing music. Whereas I could barely stay in the room for longer than five minutes before it became too much.

He really was a good guy, and there I was lusting after his ex-girlfriend like a horny teenager. But I couldn't help it. My gaze lifted to Harper again.

She was facing us, her phone pressed to one ear, and even from this distance, I could tell something was wrong. I sat forward, preparing to go to her if I thought she needed me. Needed me for what, I didn't know. But she was pinching her bottom lip, and her eyebrows were furrowed in confusion.

Almost as if sensing me watching her, she looked up and focused her eyes on me as she hung up the phone. Her lips moved, and I could tell she was saying something to the others. Goodbye, most likely, because then she jogged up the beach toward the porch where Jack had just burst through the door.

"Mrs. Kellerman. Ravishing as always," he said and dropped onto the top step.

"Hello, Jack. How is the party?"

"Well, they're getting ready for a midnight surf, so I'm here for the view." He winked, and Mrs. K laughed.

Harper approached and slowed her steps.

"Harper, good news. The guys are going for a surf," Jack announced.

She half smiled but still hadn't moved her eyes from mine. "Uh…sorry. I have to go."

"Oh, so soon? Is everything okay, dear?" my mother asked.

"Yeah. Umm, no. I just…" She bit her lip and swallowed. "I really need a…friend," she said, putting extra emphasis so I knew she needed me.

"Nate, you've not had much to drink. Why don't you take Harper home?" my mother suggested helpfully when Harper darted through the door.

"Sure." I rose to my feet then leaned down and pressed a kiss to Mum's head.

"I'll cover for you," she whispered conspiratorially.

I pulled back and stared at her, wondering how she knew these things. She was like that growing up. She always knew we'd done something before we had the courage to tell her. Half the time, she knew things about us before we did.

153

"Go." She ushered me away.

With a quick goodbye to Jack, I chased after Harper. Linc, Ryder, and Brody were grabbing boards and getting ready for a surf, while everyone else still partied. Linc's parents were in the corner chatting with my dad. The guys Linc worked with were having too much fun with the keg. I said bye to the guys as they walked out the door, not stopping to explain where I was going because I had no clue where Harper had gone and needed to find her.

It didn't take long. In fact, she found me, jumping out of the shadows when I neared my car.

One look at her face and I knew something wasn't right.

"What's wrong, friend?"

She wrapped her arms around me and buried her face in my chest. I looked over my shoulder to make sure no one could see and pressed a kiss to the top of her head.

"Let's get out of here, yeah? Then you can tell me about it."

"Okay."

I opened the car door and waited for her to get in before closing it and jogging around to my side.

Once we were away from The Love Shack and she still hadn't spoken, I decided to break the silence.

"How did your exam go yesterday?"

"Good, I think." She was quiet and withdrawn. Lost in her own thoughts. I reached across the console and grabbed her hand.

Bringing it to my lips, I pressed a kiss on each

knuckle and asked again, "What's wrong?"

"Johnny called." She took a deep breath and shifted in her seat to face me. "He received a phone call tonight and was trying to work out how to tell me. After a while, he figured it best if he just called and got it out of the way."

"And?" I glanced at her as I turned the car onto the street where my apartment was. I didn't ask if she wanted to go home because I wanted her to stay with me. She looked lost and broken on the beach after she spoke to her uncle, and an overwhelming need to protect her, comfort her, and cherish her took over.

"My brother's out."

The revelation hung in the air between us. I pulled the car over out the front of my apartment, and I unclipped both our seat belts so I could face her properly.

"Out?"

"Early release."

"When?"

"Johnny was unsure of the date, but he thinks it's been a while. Maybe even a year."

I didn't know what to say. I cupped her face in my hands and searched her eyes for a clue as to how she was feeling. Happy. Relieved. Sad. Angry. I couldn't tell.

"Who called Johnny?"

"Jeremy, but he didn't give Johnny much information. Just wanted to check on me, make sure I was safe and happy."

"He cares, Harper. He cares about you."

"But he didn't contact me. He didn't ask to visit.

155

He just wanted to know I was okay. That's it. Why?"

"I don't know. I honestly don't. Maybe he was waiting for the right time. Maybe he was scared. You'll never know unless you talk to him. Maybe you can call him. Ask Johnny for his number or something."

She laughed bitterly and pulled from my grasp. Pushing the door open, she climbed out and stomped up the steps and inside my building.

I followed her and opened the door to my apartment, letting her in.

"Harper?" I asked when she stormed down the hall to my room and began taking off her shoes.

"What?" Her dress was next. Dropped in a pool of silvery material at her feet.

I closed my bedroom door and stepped over to her, grabbing her arms as they twisted behind her back to unhook her bra.

"Stop." I said and brought her hands down in front of her. The moment I let them go, they went straight behind her back again.

"Stop trying to undress yourself," I said, pulling her arms back in between us again.

She reached for my shirt and began undoing the buttons. "Fine, I'll undress you."

"Stop trying to get us naked." I couldn't believe I actually said that to her. What guy in his right mind would turn her down? I couldn't resist her for three months, and now she was standing in front of me in nothing but her underwear, tugging my pants down my legs.

What happened to my shirt?

"Can't have sex with clothes on, Nate," she said and crouched to remove my shoes and pants at the same time.

"You're angry. We are not having sex."

Damn my conscience to hell. There I went again. Turning her down. But it was the right thing to do. She was angry and hurting that her brother, who she idolised and looked up to, was a free man and hadn't made any effort to contact her.

"But didn't you know, friend? Angry sex is the best kind." She reached behind her back and unhooked her bra.

I tried hard. Really hard not to look. And I didn't...for all of three seconds. I was only human. And a man, at that. And putting a beautiful, half-naked woman in front of a man and asking him not to look was like dangling fine whiskey in front of an alcoholic and telling them don't touch. Laughable.

So, I looked.

I followed her curves with my gaze, letting my eyes wander over the softness of her skin. The swell of her breasts. Her tight, toned stomach. The tiny scrap of black lace that barely passed for underwear. My mouth was dry, and all the blood in my body was heading south. But it wasn't the time.

I scooped up my shirt from the bed and draped it around her shoulders, helping her to slide her arms in, and then I picked her up and placed her in my bed, much like I did the other night. I climbed in behind her and wrapped my arm around her waist and kissed the top of her shoulder.

"Why would he not contact me?" she asked.

"There could be a dozen reasons, and you'll

157

never know unless you ask."

She rolled over and faced me, and her fingers danced along my cheekbones. "Would you come with me?"

"If you want me to, yes."

"Thank you." She smiled and brought her face to mine. Her tongue darted out and licked my bottom lip. With a playful look in her eyes, she asked, "Now, about that angry sex?"

I grabbed her by waist and rolled her on top of me. A surprised squeal left her lips, and she giggled.

The sound of the front door slamming shut echoed through the apartment, and I quickly placed my hand over Harper's mouth to stop her from making noise.

What the hell was Brody doing home already?

Harper rolled off me and froze, too scared to move in case Brody heard her. I pulled her back to my chest and wrapped an arm around her waist and waited for Brody to go to bed, but he had other ideas.

The bathroom door opened. The toilet flushed. The tap ran. Lights off. Lights on. Doors opening and closing. Footsteps up and down the hall. The fridge opened. A glass clinked. Liquid sloshed. The crackle of a chip packet being opened. All the while, we lay motionless, while I tried not to think about Harper's ass pressing into me or the way her heart was beating seemingly in time with mine.

Finally, after the longest and most tense wait, the TV turned on. It meant we could relax a little. He wouldn't hear us if he was watching something.

I brushed Harper's hair to the side and pressed a

kiss behind her ear. She sighed and gripped my hand around her waist, fast asleep.

Chapter Sixteen

Harper

I woke in the morning to featherlight kisses behind my ear. My shirt unbuttoned, and his fingers brushed my stomach, over my ribs, tickling as they went until they reached the collar of the shirt and tugged it down over my shoulder. I sat up and allowed Nate to remove it completely. I had given in entirely. I was kidding myself when I said it was one night only. The man was irresistible.

Looking at him over my shoulder, he still appeared to be half asleep. He smiled up at me and leaned forward to press a kiss to my spine. I shivered from the coolness of his lips on my overheated skin. He pulled me back down on the mattress and rolled until he hovered above me. "Good morning, friend."

"We're still using that line, are we?" I gasped and tilted my head back, driving my fingers into his hair when his tongue glided down the column of my throat until his teeth nipped at my collarbone. Why was that so sexy?

"Well, you're my friend..."

"Friends don't sleep naked next to each other."

"Who's naked? I'm wearing boxers, so who else have you been sharing a bed with?" he teased, gliding a hand down my side to my hip. His fingers dug into my flesh, massaging, kneading, caressing.

"Just you. I—" I froze and stared wide-eyed at Nate's door, waiting.

Brody's door had just opened and closed. He was home. I assumed he'd have gone out or something. Nate's lips continued their delicious assault on my skin, skimming down my stomach until he paused and lifted his gaze to meet mine, a cheeky smile on his gorgeous face.

"Roll over?"

"What?"

"Roll over." When I didn't move, he sat back on his knees and flipped me onto my stomach. "That's better."

He braced his hands on either side of me. I tensed, my body and ears on high alert. What was he doi—?

His tongue flicked my lower back, once, twice, three times on one side before moving to the other side and doing it all over again.

"Told you I wanted to lick those dimples." He flipped me back over and—

A knock sounded at the door.

Nate cursed, staring at me with wide, panicked eyes. Crap. What did I do? If Brody walked in, we were dead. How could we be so stupid? This was a terrible idea. Awful. Big mistake. *Huge* mistake.

161

Then why did it feel so right?

Making a quick decision, one that would have most girls feeling self-conscious and embarrassed, I slid off the mattress and onto the floor, hiding myself between the bed and the window. Brody wouldn't have a clue I was there unless he walked around the room or peered under the bed.

Nate snatched up my dress and shoes and threw them under the bed before climbing back under the covers and casually throwing an arm over the side, right where I was lying.

We waited in silence for Brody to leave or walk in. Nate's hand was conveniently on my breast, squeezing gently, rubbing. I pushed it away, and he chuckled softly, using his pillow to muffle the sound, before returning his hand to continue touching my sensitive flesh.

Brody knocked again and called out Nate's name. The door opened, and I held my breath, not wanting to make a noise. Nate increased the pressure of his hand, massaging my breast, his thumb brushing my nipple. My eyes rolled back, and I bit my lip to stop myself from moaning. It felt amazing.

"Nate?" Brody whispered, and when Nate didn't answer, Brody pulled the door closed. Neither of us moved for a minute. We listened to make sure Brody had left, and the instant we heard the fridge door open, Nate was off the bed and on me, pulling his pillows down on the floor with him.

His lips met mine in a frenzied, hurried kiss. Our teeth clashed together, our tongues sliding against one another while our hands fumbled with our underwear. My heart was beating out of my chest. Brody was just down the hall. He could hear us at any moment, but that made it so much more exciting. The risk.

Rising to his feet, Nate discarded his boxer shorts, leaving him gloriously naked in front of me. My underwear practically fell off by itself. Combusted. Gone. Like magic. He positioned the pillows in a row and lifted me onto them. Leaning over me, he reached into his side table and pulled out a condom.

Kenzie's voice echoed in my head, *safety first*, and I chuckled.

Worst time to start laughing.

"Something funny, friend?" he whispered.

"No…" I took a deep breath as he settled his body over me. "Not funny at all."

"Good." Nate pulled my lip between his teeth and nudged my legs open.

Finding my hands and entwining our fingers, he kissed me. Slow, languid movements as his tongue explored my mouth. I lifted my hips to meet his as he eased himself into me, taking his time. Dragging it out. My back arched, needing to feel closer as I moaned at the feeling of him moving inside me. The warmth of his skin sliding against mine. Too warm, but still not enough. Our mouths fused together, breathing each other's air, stifling our moans.

I wanted to touch him.

Explore his body.

Run my fingers through his hair.

Scratch my nails down his back.

But I couldn't. My hands were pinned. I was

163

completely at his mercy.

Moving his mouth from mine, kissing my jaw, my neck, caressing my lips with his, Nate's eyes sought mine. Hazy with lust, our gazes locked, watching every emotion, every thought flicker as the slow, deliberate, and gentle movement of his hips rocking into mine built a pleasure that sent us spiralling over the edge.

***

We fell back asleep, wrapped in each other's arms on the floor. Something had shifted. I felt it in the way Nate held me. I saw it in his eyes. I felt it in my bones. In my heart. There was no going back, no matter the consequences. No matter the fallout. For six months, I had tried to fight my attraction to him. Evidently, I failed epically for three of those months. But there was no fighting it. It couldn't be stopped. We were tied together by an invisible thread. A strong, unbreakable thread. A chain. With padlocks.

I combed my fingers through his hair and watched his chest rise and fall with every breath. Nate lifted his sleepy head and smiled at me lazily. "Hi, friend."

"Hi," I said quietly, conscious of Brody in the next room. We stared at each other with our lips pulled up into cheesy grins. My heart fluttered. He was so beautiful it almost hurt to look at him, but I did. A lot. He was like a fine—very fine—piece of artwork. Sculptors should model all their masterpieces on him. "What are you doing today?"

Nate inched higher until his mouth brushed mine. "You," he whispered against my lips.

My eyelids fluttered closed. "I'm totally okay with that," I murmured, lifting my chin and kissing him. I wanted to bottle his kisses, his scent, his essence and take him with me wherever I went. I felt like Alice, falling down the rabbit hole, and Nate was my Wonderland.

Voices sounded in the living room. Garbled at first, I couldn't understand the words they were saying. Nate groaned and dropped his head to my chest, and then Linc's husky voice rang loud and clear as it got closer to the bedroom door.

"I'll get him."

My eyes widened in shock. Linc was going to walk in that door any second, and I was naked on the floor.

Pressing a soft kiss to my shoulder, he stood and held out his hand, telling me to stay hidden. "This isn't over."

I hoped not.

He pulled his shorts on just as the door opened. I lay perfectly still. Again.

"Oh, you're up," Brody said.

"Well spotted." Linc laughed. "We're going to play a game of basketball down by the beach. Get dressed. Let's go."

"Uh, nah, you guys go ahead without me," Nate said, his tone uneven. I could picture the scene. He'd be rubbing his neck nervously, and Linc would be watching him with curious eyes.

"Come on, man, get out of the house a little. I'm gonna get changed now. Give me five minutes."

165

Brody's footsteps retreated down the hall, and I breathed a sigh of relief.

"Seriously, you need to get out. Have some fun. Work out your frustrations," Linc said.

"Believe me, I have well and truly worked out my frustrations today." Nate cleared his throat. "Lots of fun."

We worked out both our frustrations today. I giggled and quickly slapped my hand over my mouth. I couldn't believe I did that.

Dammit.

Did Linc hear?

"Who was that?"

"Shh, keep your voice down. You need to get him out of here," Nate said.

"Who?"

The door closed gently, and the sound of water running in the bathroom drifted through the walls. It wasn't the shower, though, just a tap, which meant Brody was likely brushing his teeth.

"Brody. Get him out of the house. I need a little more time."

"Nah, don't think I will. Not until you tell me why your bed giggled."

Jeez, Linc was stubborn. I sat up, careful to keep my naked body hidden behind the bed and waved at Linc.

"Fucking frustrations." Linc threw his hands in the air and turned away. "Fine. But you get her out of here the moment we're gone."

"Thanks, man. I'll meet you at the beach."

"I hope you both know what you're doing," Linc said, shaking his head. He opened the door and walked out, being sure to close it behind him.

Neither of us moved until the front door slammed shut, no doubt from Linc.

"Fucking frustrations."

I laughed as I got to my feet and walked around the bed in search of my clothes. Nate grabbed my hips and pulled me to him.

"What are you doing?" His breath was warm on my neck.

"Getting my clothes." I moaned and tilted my head to the side when his mouth found that curve between my neck and shoulder and began sucking.

"Why?"

"You heard Linc. They'll be waiting for you."

His chest rubbed against my back, and he brought his hand up my body, sliding it around my neck until finally he grasped the side of my head and turned it to face him. "They can wait. I told you this wasn't over." And then his mouth was on mine. Hot, needy, demanding. I melted in his arms, completely at his mercy for the second time that day.

Nate dropped me home a little while later, dressed in gym shorts and a tank, ready to meet the guys at the basketball courts by the beach. We spent fifteen minutes making out like teenagers parked in his car out the front of the diner where anyone could have seen. But we didn't care. I didn't care.

I knew when I climbed out of his car, leaving him with one last kiss, that over the course of the last two weeks I had inadvertently given him my fragile heart to protect.

It was a risk, but it was worth it.

I just didn't know the risk I'd be taking so soon.

CHAPTER
SEVENTEEN

Nate

Linc pulled me aside after the game once everyone had left. Ryder had gone to meet Bailey, and Brody was heading to see Audrey. He slapped me over the back of the head, causing me to choke on the water I had just swallowed.

I rubbed the spot he hit and growled. "What was that for?"

"For thinking with your dick."

"What?"

"Harper. Seriously. Of all the chicks you could smooth talk your way into bed, you had to choose her. I hope you know what you're doing." He tossed the basketball at me.

"It's not like that." I bounced the ball a couple of times.

"Well, by all means, enlighten me." Linc lifted his arms in a wide gesture then sat on the hot court.

The sun was scorching today, burning the back of my neck.

"I don't know, man. It's just not. It's not a casual thing," I said and sat in front of him, the ball between my legs.

"You know Brody is still in love with her, right?"

I nodded. I knew, and that was why it was so hard to admit.

"So am I."

"Well, shit." Linc barked out a laugh and slapped his hands on his knees. "You got yourself in a hell of a mess."

"I know. But I can't let her walk away this time."

"You sure about that?"

"Would you willingly walk away from Indie?"

"Hell, no," he growled, his eyes narrowing and a scowl forming on his face from the mere thought.

"There you go." I shrugged.

"So, what are you going to do?"

I thought about it for a moment and laughed. "Set Brody up."

Linc paused, his eyes squinted in concentration before he slanted his head to the side and shrugged. "Not a terrible idea."

"I wasn't serious." I threw the ball and hit him hard in the chest. He caught it, but the force knocked him backwards.

"What? It could work. If he moves on, he won't care *as much* that you're sticking it to his ex."

"Sticking it to his—" I shook my head in disbelief. "Who even says that?"

"I know." Linc dropped his head. "Spend too

170

much time with Jack, and he rubs off on you...or against you. Literally. Seriously. There's no boundaries with that guy."

"Jack arrived two days ago." He couldn't have that much of an effect on Linc already.

"Believe me. I am well aware. He is everywhere. All the time."

"Least you know what to expect with him. Anything and everything."

"Okay, back to Brody. Do we know any single women?" He was scheming now.

"None."

"There's gotta be someone."

"He doesn't have time to date anyone, anyway."

"Why the hell not?"

"Between working and spending nearly every other minute sitting in that hospital room with Audrey, he's hardly home."

"He was home today," Linc pointed out helpfully.

"Yes. I know."

He laughed. "You guys have balls, that's for sure. Huge risk bringing Harper to your place. I mean, really."

He was right. It was stupid, but I'd do it again. And again.

I smiled.

"You're in so deep," he said, checking his watch, and then cursed. "We have to go."

"Why?"

"Dinner at your parents'. They'll kill us if we're late."

I'd almost forgotten about the weekly dinners,

and I really didn't want to go, but then my stomach rumbled at the thought of food.

"Good, I'm hungry."

***

It seemed I missed the memo that my parents were cooking dinner for everyone. I pulled my car to the side of the street because their drive was full, and I had nowhere to park.

Opening the front door, laughter rang through the house. I walked through to the kitchen, and Mum was standing behind the counter preparing a salad.

"Need help?"

"Nate." She smiled and gave me her cheek when I leaned in to kiss her. "No, go on outside with everyone. Relax."

"You sure?"

"Of course. It's just something light. Your father's out by the barbecue." She nodded in the direction of the French doors.

"Okay."

"What took you so long?" Indie asked when I stepped onto the patio. She was sitting around the table with Kenzie, Bailey, and Jack, a bottle of wine between them. Linc was standing with my dad watching Ryder flip burgers on the grill. Cole was splashing in the pool.

Honest answer? I was obsessed with a particular fair-skinned, raven-haired beauty. I swung by the diner on the way home to see Harper. And a good thing I had too. Johnny had said she came home and demanded to know where her brother was and how she could contact him. It took a lot of arguing on her part, but Johnny eventually gave up Jeremy's number, and Harper called him. She was in full-blown panic mode, on edge, nervous and jittery. He agreed to meet with her next Tuesday. Just to talk. But, there was no chance in hell I would let her go alone.

I couldn't.

What if he told her he never wanted to see her again?

What if he had changed from the teenage boy she remembered?

What if he was dangerous?

I couldn't let her go alone.

"Nate?"

"Huh?"

"What took you so long? We've been here for an hour."

"I had things to do. I have a life, you know."

Indie scoffed. "You do not." And then her eyes brightened, and she clapped her hands. "I have an idea."

I eyed her warily and folded my arms. I didn't like her ideas. What was with this group and their scheming ways? "What?" I asked hesitantly.

She leaned forward with a smile and placed her wineglass on the table. "I'm going to set you up!"

"No." I shook my head. "No way." Shook it again for reinforcement. "I can get my own dates."

"You haven't had a girlfriend for two years. Clearly, you're doing something wrong. Linc told me about your plan to find Brody a girlfriend, so

173

let's find you one too."

Kenzie watched me curiously.

"Just because you finally have your first boyfriend does not mean you're a matchmaker or an expert," I said.

"Fiancé." She wiggled the diamond in my face. "And maybe it does. Maybe I just know how to pick 'em. Soulmate radar."

I tipped my head back and laughed. "Soulmate radar. What is wrong with you?"

"I got Bailey and Ryder together, didn't I?" she said, a smug smile on her face.

"Ah…" Bailey raised her hand, her head tilted to the side and her eyebrows furrowed in confusion. "You did not."

"I totally did."

"Are you crazy?"

"No. I'm Indie." She waved Bailey off. "Whatever. If it weren't for me, you never would have admitted you were in love with him."

"I would so." Bailey rolled her eyes and poured more wine.

"Psssh, you thought you were fake dating, when it was clear to even Blind Freddy that it was real. I specifically remember making you realise you had real feelings for your super-hot boyfriend."

Linc whipped his head around at that statement, a scowl on his face. Ryder just laughed.

"You might want retract that statement, Ace," Linc growled, slamming his beer on the table and walking over to her.

"Not as hot as you, stupid ass." Indie rolled her eyes and tipped her head back when Linc grabbed her face and claimed her mouth.

"One day, I will understand the meaning of those nicknames," I muttered.

"Oh, I know!" Jack hollered. "Ace is because she's a great kisser. Well, duh." He flicked his hands at himself. "Great teacher. I should charge. And stupid ass is what Indie said when she told Linc she loved him."

"Huh?"

"I believe it went something like this," Jack said and cleared his throat, facing an invisible person on his left. 'Hey, Linc, is Indie a good kisser?'" Then he changed the direction he faced, and in his best Linc-inspired voice said, "'Yeah, she's Ace.'" He shot a wink at Linc and gave him a thumbs up.

"Right," I said slowly. Kenzie and Bailey were trying not to laugh behind their hands, while Ryder ignored him and focused on taking the meat inside.

"And then the bombshell dropped. They were fighting on the beach because my plan was just that good. And Indie turned and shoved him away." Jack brushed his imaginary long hair and pouted, trying terribly to imitate Indie, then in a high-pitched voice said, "'Because I love you, you stupid ass.'" Then he cleared his throat and used the deep voice for Linc. "'Say it again?'" Switched back to Indie. "'Stupid ass?'"

Yeah, that totally sounded like Indie.

"Then they made sweet, sweet love on the beach in front of the entire resort."

My hands balled into fists. My jaw set.

"Knock it off. We did not." Linc punched his shoulder.

175

"Ouch. Pick on someone your own size." Jack laughed. "No. They didn't, I swear. He didn't steal her virtue right away. He waited a day."

A growl erupted in my throat.

"All right. Enough. Jack, stop trying to work Nate up." Dad stepped in, laying a hand on Jack's shoulder.

"Dinner's ready," Mum announced, holding the doors open for Ryder as he returned carrying two trays of freshly made burgers. And I'd be damned if they didn't look and smell better than Johnny's.

"Cole, come on," Kenzie called and got up to help Cole dry off and fix him some food.

"Ugh, Mumma… Stop." He shook his head and tried to get out from under the towel she was using to dry his hair.

"Where's Brody? I thought he was coming," Dad asked as he pulled out a chair for Mum. After all these years, they were still romantic and kind and loving toward each other.

"He was going to the hospital again," I said and grabbed a burger and took a huge bite. Juice dripped down my chin and fingers, but Ryder wasn't lying. His burgers kicked Johnny's ass.

Dad cleared his throat and glanced at my mother, who reached over and patted his hand reassuringly.

"What's going on?" I asked, watching them carefully.

"Well, I guess now is as good as any time," Dad said, taking a mouthful of his beer. "We wanted to speak to the four of you, but…"

"Four?" Indie asked.

"Yes. You and Nate, obviously. Lincoln, son,

because you're just as much family as our own, and Brody because it will affect him as well."

Silence fell over the table.

"We'll give you a minute," Bailey said and pushed her chair out.

"Nonsense. Sit back down. You'll all find out soon enough," my mother said, pointing at Bailey's chair. She dropped back into it silently.

"Your mother and I have decided to have another child."

I choked on my beer. Indie sprayed wine all over herself, and everyone else was too stunned to even blink, let alone speak. My eyes found Indie's, her face betraying every thought she had. Linc leaned back in his chair and rested his arm around her waist. Bailey's mouth was twisted, and her eyes narrowed. Ryder, once again, was blank. No expression. No reaction. The dude had a killer poker face. Kenzie busied herself with Cole, pretending not to have heard, and Jack looked like he'd seen a ghost. Face white, hands slapped on his cheeks, his mouth open in a silent scream. Exactly like I felt.

"Come again?" I asked.

Another child. A kid? What the hell? They couldn't have another child. Pretty sure that ship had well and truly sailed, medically, at least. Were they adopting? Why would they want one? Holy shit.

"We're lonely. The house is empty. We just don't know what to do with ourselves anymore."

"Join a club. Ride a bike. Take a class. Pottery. Golf. Hell, do yoga with Bailey's mother. Music lessons. Travel. Anything!" I suggested and looked to Indie for support, but she was still sitting there wide-eyed. She was no help.

"We love you both, so much, and if we can provide for another child in need the way we did you, then that would mean something."

"You're really serious?" Linc asked.

"Immensely."

"I think that's a lovely thing to do." Bailey smiled. Ryder nodded in agreement.

"Thank you, Bailey."

"Oh. My. God...I'm going to be a big sister!" Indie squealed, a look of wonder on her face. "I've always wanted a little brother or sister. I can teach him to ride a bike and play basketball—fairly." She elbowed Linc and stuck her tongue out at me.

"Indie," my dad said.

"Or I can teach her how braid her hair and make dresses look really cute with Chucks." Her eyes widened.

"Indie," Dad tried again.

"I can buy her first pair of Chucks. She'll be a mini me."

"Indie."

"What?"

"Listen, please. Your father and I have seen a lawyer and are going through the process of fostering a young lady." My mother's eyes glistened with tears. My dad squeezed her hand, and they both looked at me with sad smiles. "We hired someone to look into the girl's background. She's an orphan. No family. Her parents immigrated here from Italy before she was born."

My stomach dropped. I shook my head.

"Our lawyer is taking care of everything. Dealing with child services and pushing our application through as fast as possible."

"Why the rush?" Jack asked. My hands were clammy. Sweat prickled at the nape of my neck.

"The girl. She has no one. And pretty soon the place she is staying will no longer be able to care for her. She'll be placed into foster care, and she'll get lost in the system. Her needs are great. She will need help with everyday things. Things that come naturally to others. She'll need doctor visits and therapist visits. So much that we can provide for her. We want to provide for her. Give her the best care possible."

"What's wrong with her?" Indie whispered. Linc shifted in his seat uncomfortably and glanced at me. He knew. He'd figured it out.

I wiped my hands on my shorts and closed my eyes. I didn't want to see their faces when they found out who my parents were adopting.

"She's a burn victim," Dad said sadly.

"Audrey," I croaked and opened my eyes to look at my parents.

"Audrey." My mother sniffed. "Nate, it's the right thing."

I stood from the table and walked toward the door, stopping to kiss her on the head. "I know. I just need time to sort through some things, and you need to make sure you're not rushing into this. It is a huge responsibility."

"We know. And we're prepared. We've discussed this long and hard. We've got everything in motion. We just need to speak with Audrey first.

179

She's not a child and obviously will have a say in what happens. But we can't bear the thought of her being put into the foster system. So many of those families are in it for the money, and they don't really care about the kids. We do. We want to help her," my dad said.

I nodded then shook my head. I was confused. A thousand thoughts swirled through my mind. "I have to go."

I walked out the door and got in my car.

CHAPTER EIGHTEEN

Harper

I was watching television with Julie. Nothing terribly exciting, just mindless stuff I didn't have to concentrate on. Which was perfect because all I could think about was my brother and how he'd sounded exactly the same on the phone earlier as he did the last time I saw him.

I kept replaying our last conversation in my head. Him telling me to go and not come back. It still didn't make sense to me why he would do that. He'd spent his entire life looking out for me.

What changed?

And I then I began to wonder whether he resented, blamed me for his life in prison. If he hadn't been in a rush to save me from the clutches of my parents, he wouldn't have been speeding. He would have seen the kid out on the road. He would have had time to stop. The kid would be alive, and

181

my brother and I would have been living a glamorous life somewhere far, far away. He wouldn't have spent eight years in prison and pushed me away when he'd had enough. He wouldn't have made parole and not reached out to me.

My phone buzzed in my pocket, pulling me away from the show I wasn't even watching. Taking it out, I saw a text from Nate.

Nate: Stars are bright tonight.

The stars were bright. A little cryptic, but okay.

Harper: Aren't they always?

Why was he texting me about the stars?

Nate: Can see the Milky Way.

And then I knew. I grabbed a blanket from the back of the sofa and told Julie I was heading outside. She waved me off, too engrossed in the drama unfolding on the television.

Johnny was cleaning the kitchen in the diner when I darted out the back door and through the field behind the roadhouse to the water tower.

"Hi, friend," Nate said from the shadows, causing me to jump. I spun on my heels and wrapped my arms around his neck.

"Hi," I said, leaning in to kiss him. "What are you doing here?"

"I needed a friend."

He looked tired and drawn, but that couldn't be. He slept last night and most of the day. But something was off.

I pulled him to the ladder of the tower and climbed up silently with him following.

"Talk to me," I said, settling back against the tank and taking Nate's hand.

"My parents want to foster Audrey."

I surely heard that wrong. Where did that come from?

"Audrey? As in, Audrey?"

"Yep."

"How are you with that?"

"I don't really know." He sighed and brought our joined hands up to his mouth, pressing kisses on each of my knuckles. "I love that they care and they want to help her. And they can. She's got a long recovery, and they'll get her the best doctors and the best treatment they possibly can. I hated the thought of her being alone, orphaned with nowhere to live and no one to love her."

I squeezed his hand gently and rested my head on his shoulder.

"But I don't know if I can walk into their house once a week, if not more, and see her there. I can barely get through a five-minute hospital visit with her, and she's not even awake. The guilt would eat me alive. Does that make me a bad person?"

"Of course not. That doesn't make you a bad person. It makes you human." I climbed onto my knees and straddled his legs. Grabbing his face in my hands, I held him there until he looked at me. "It makes you a human who is feeling incredibly guilty

183

about a tragedy that was completely out of his control. And that's okay."

"You think?"

"Yes. You'll finish your therapy sessions, working through your fear and guilt, and soon enough, everything will go back to normal. And you'll walk into your parents' house, and you'll see Audrey, and you'll smile and sit with her, and you'll be her protective older brother, giving her hell and chasing away all the boys who look in her direction."

Nate took a deep breath and smiled, and then frowned. "She better not have boys knocking on the front door."

I laughed. "See, overprotective already."

"I guess you're right."

"I always am, friend."

"But what if she doesn't want to live with my parents? They are so set on the idea of bringing her home, I don't think they've considered the fact she might not want to live with them. Or if she does, she'll be eighteen soon enough and might want to leave then."

"As for your parents, that's something they need to think about. She's fragile now and needs a lot of care, but she's almost an adult who will certainly want to assert her independence. But speaking from experience, had your parents been around when I was in foster care, I would have jumped at the chance to live with them. The places I lived, the families who took me in were awful. They need to spend time with her. Get to know her. And let her make the decision." I knew without a doubt that living with Nate's parents would be Audrey's best option if she truly had no relatives to care for her.

"You're pretty smart, you know." He smiled.

"I have my moments."

"So, can we just make out for, like, five or six hours?" he asked, slipping his hands into the waistband of my shorts.

"Thought you'd never ask."

***

I was a nervous wreck. My hands were shaking, and I had this uncontrollable twitch in my eye that made it constantly look like I was winking. I wasn't.

Aunt Julie had cleaned the same table six times now. At least she was trying to be discreet, unlike Uncle Johnny, who was leaning against the wall with his arms folded across his chest and a meat cleaver dangling from his fingers.

Nate had a death grip on my hand under the table while rubbing reassuring circles on my thigh with the other.

"I've missed you," Jeremy said, lifting his mug of coffee to his lips. His eyes crinkled at the corners as he winced when the scalding liquid ran down his throat. His cropped hair was a stark contrast to the shaggy black hair he had when we were growing up.

I searched his face, taking in every detail, every frown line. Every scar—there were a lot, and not just on his face. His arms were littered with various white scars, only to be disguised by the multitude of tattoos covering practically every square inch of his skin that was on display.

"I've missed you too," I admitted.

"And who's this?" Jeremy dragged his caramel eyes over to Nate, inspecting him carefully.

"This is Nate."

"Your boyfriend?"

I shot a panicked look at Nate. I didn't know what to say. We hadn't classified our relationship yet.

"Just friends," Nate said with ease.

Discomfort settled in my stomach, and a chill washed over my body. Just friends.

Just friends.

We weren't just friends.

Just friends didn't share a bed every single night.

Just friends didn't sneak around behind everyone's back, stealing kisses and touches when no one was paying attention.

Just friends didn't have sex together.

Not against the front door.

Or on the stairs at the diner.

Or in the other friend's parents' swimming pool while the parents sat inside, barely twenty feet away.

Just friends didn't make love in the back seat of the car on a deserted road by the beach.

Or quietly in the shower when the roommate was in the next room.

And they sure as hell didn't make love on a water tower under the stars.

Twice.

Just friends weren't so stupidly, blindly attracted

to each other that when they were together all common sense was lost.

Just friends didn't throw caution to the wind and say *screw the consequences*.

Just friends.

My ass.

We were so much more than just friends.

I shifted in my seat, putting some space between Nate and me. If we were just friends, we shouldn't be sitting so close. He shot me a look that basically said "what are you doing?"

"Yeah. Friends." Nate noticed the tone of my voice had hardened. His mouth turned down in a frown.

"Are you happy?" Jeremy asked.

I had been happy. Until two minutes ago.

"Yes." I smiled, tried to make it look believable. "How are you adjusting?"

I was concerned for my brother. Being free after eight years in prison for an accident that could have been avoided was a huge adjustment. I had so many questions I wanted to ask him, but I couldn't sort through my thoughts.

"Okay. Just looking for work."

"Where are you living?"

"Moving from place to place. Wherever the work takes me, I guess."

"Why did you send me away that day?" I didn't mean to blurt out the question like that, but it was the one thing I needed to know, to understand more than anything.

"That was the hardest thing I had ever done in my life. But I was scared. I was scared you were

187

going to follow us down the dead-end path. You were young, bright, had your entire future ahead of you but stayed around for me. I didn't want to hold you back. I didn't want to cause you pain. I wanted you to have this life. The one where you're happy and doing something you're passionate about. I didn't want to burden you with my woes."

"But don't you see? You did. You did burden me with your woes. You did cause me pain. So much pain. All I wanted was my brother. I didn't care the only way I could have you was from behind a glass wall. I didn't care that I couldn't touch you or hug you. I just wanted to be there for you. And you stopped seeing me."

Tears flowed freely. Unstoppable.

"I wanted to make it up to you. I wanted you to forgive me for being the reason you were in prison in the first place." My chest tightened, restricting my breathing. It hurt to finally get everything off my chest.

"Hey. No." Jeremy was out of his seat and pulling me into his arms in a second. "Don't think for one second any of that was on you. I chose to come looking for you. I chose to speed. They fucked up and chose drugs over their daughter. It was their fault."

"You really don't blame me."

"I really don't blame you. I'm sorry. So sorry for everything I've done. Do you think one day we'll get past it?"

"Already forgotten." I smiled into his chest and held him tight. "Have you heard from them?"

"Who?" He stiffened and released me.

I gave him a look that said "you know who."

"No. Not since that last morning I went to work, only to come home and find your note. They could be dead in a gutter, for all I care."

I nodded in agreement. They weren't parents. I had no feelings toward them any longer. They meant nothing. Less than nothing.

All I cared about was getting my brother back.

CHAPTER NINETEEN

Nate

Jeremy stayed in town for a couple of days. And I'd never seen Harper so relaxed. Happy. She was enjoying catching up and spending time with her brother after so long. He had her full attention, and I barely saw her, but that was okay. She needed this time with him.

I was sitting on the sofa watching TV, bored out of my brain and refusing to speak to Indie because she kept trying to set me up on dates, when Brody walked in. Everyone was busy at work, and I was itching to get back myself, but Cap still had me on suspension. Apparently, my therapist didn't think I was ready to return yet, even though I was sleeping now. According to her, using Harper as a sleeping aid wasn't helping me get over the fire, and I still had to work through my feelings.

Whatever.

"She's awake," Brody said the moment he walked through the door.

"Huh?"

"Audrey. She's awake."

My blood ran cold, and my stomach flipped. I wanted to throw up. Instead, I nodded and changed the channels.

"Well?"

"What?" I rubbed my temples, feeling a headache forming. She was awake. She was going to find out she had lost her entire family, that I couldn't save them. My chest tightened, and I swallowed.

"Are you coming with me to see her?"

"I don't think I can." I rubbed my chest and tried to steady my breathing.

"I think you should."

I didn't think I could face her. Not yet. It was hard enough to see her when she was asleep. But now, to see the pain in her eyes, the lost expression on her face…

"I can't."

I wasn't ready. Plain and simple.

"Okay." Brody turned and walked back out the door, no doubt headed straight to the hospital.

I grabbed a beer from the fridge and returned to the sofa and the TV. Images of Audrey in the hospital bed, or under wet towels in the remains of the bathroom flashed through my mind. I had to see her. I knew that. I just couldn't handle seeing her yet. I didn't want to be there when she found out what happened. I wasn't chickening out. I'd go and see her in a few days, when she'd had time to process everything. When I had time to process everything.

I was still in the same spot six hours later when Brody returned, only I had a lot more empty beer bottles on the coffee table.

"Dude?" He eyed the table and raised an eyebrow. "Party for one?"

I grunted and took another swig of beer.

"Have you moved at all today?"

"I went to the fridge." I raised my beer and waved it in front of him.

"That's it?"

I nodded. "Oh, wait. No, I went to the bathroom to take a piss. Multiple times. Broke the seal." I smiled, proud of myself for moving more than he thought.

"Are you drunk?"

"Not nearly enough."

Brody flopped into the seat beside me and tilted his head back with a groan. We sat silently for a while, me drinking my beer, and Brody staring at the ceiling until I asked the question I wasn't sure I wanted the answer to.

"How is she?"

"Scared. Heartbroken. Hurt. Sad. Lost. Confused. Numb. I don't know, man. She was quiet, in pain, and just alone." Brody sighed.

My heart plummeted. I couldn't begin to imagine how she was feeling, and I hoped to god I never had to.

"She wants to meet you," he said quietly. I wasn't even sure I heard him right.

"What?"

"I sat with her for a while, talked to her about what happened, and she wants to meet you."

"She actually spoke to you?" I was shocked. I would have thought she'd be wary of a stranger visiting her or too upset to talk.

Brody's face lit up. "Yeah. She remembered me."

"Huh?"

"She remembered my face from when we rescued her and my voice from the times I read to her."

"Right," I said. I could maybe believe she remembered his face when we carried her outside, but his voice? She was asleep the entire time.

"Strange, yeah? She said she thought she was dreaming about someone reading to her."

"Weird," I agreed. "And she wants to meet me?"

"Yep."

"Why?"

"She remembered you being there too."

"What? In her dreams?" I laughed.

"At the house, idiot."

She remembered me? I smiled and decided the least I could do was visit her. I guessed I should, if my parents were serious about taking her in as a foster child. And I was pretty sure they were, which meant I needed to help them in any way I could. If by visiting Audrey and getting to know her, making her feel comfortable around me, maybe when it was time for her to meet my parents, it wouldn't be so bad. Maybe she'd be open to the idea of living with them because Harper and my parents were right. The system was shit, and putting her into foster care

193

with an unknown family could have disastrous effects on her. My parents would give her everything she needed, and she'd be well looked after.

"I'll visit her tomorrow."

"I'll come with, if you want."

"Thanks, man," I said and stood to gather all my empty beer bottles from the coffee table. And then I turned it Brody, my drunken brain talking for me. "Do me a favour?"

"What?"

"Drop me at the roadhouse?" I asked, swaying on my feet.

"Why?"

"Because I really want to see…" Dammit. I paused, took a breath, and tried again. "Johnny. I need to see Johnny." I couldn't say Harper. I wasn't in the frame of mind for that conversation yet. I wasn't sure I ever would be.

"Johnny?"

I nodded slowly, biting my lip to stop from talking further.

"Why?"

"Food. Burgers. He makes them. I need them." I rubbed my belly.

Brody laughed and snatched his keys from the coffee table. "Let's go."

We walked into the diner. Well, Brody walked, I stumbled. The fresh air hit me and amped up the effects of those beers.

I was surprised to see a couple of customers sitting and eating at the booth and another at the counter ordering. I'd never seen anyone in here before.

Brody waved at Julie, who proceeded to shout to Johnny that she needed two more burgers for us, and then he led me over to the booth. I couldn't be trusted to walk by myself, since I didn't notice the tables and chairs on the floor in front of me.

Harper was cleaning tables, and I couldn't help but smile at the sight of her. As if she sensed me watching her, she turned and focused on me. I took a step toward her and only stopped when Brody called, "Hey, Harper."

My drunken brain almost had me walking over and kissing that pretty mouth of hers. That would have been a disaster.

She put the cloth she was using into the pocket of her apron and came over to us. "Hey."

"Hi." I smiled.

She bit her lip. "Hi."

"Hey," I said again.

"Okay." Brody clapped once. "Now we've got that weird greeting out of the way, can we sit before you fall over?" He nudged me into the booth then slid into the other side.

"Hi, friend." I rested my head on my hands and smiled up at Harper.

She narrowed her eyes and frowned. "Are you drunk?" she said before turning to Brody. "Is he drunk?"

"Yes," Brody answered, and at the same time, I shook my head.

"No. I'm Nate." I laughed at my own joke because it was funny.

"I'm getting you some water," Harper said and

walked over to the counter and returned with a bottle of water for me.

I guzzled down the water, drops sliding down my chin. I was thirstier than I thought. Harper reached a hand out and touched my jaw briefly, as though she was going to wipe the water drops away, but her eyes widened and she gasped, pulling her hand back like I'd burned her.

I frowned.

"How's your brother? Do we get to meet him?" Brody asked, oblivious to anything that was passing between Harper and me. And that might have been because the alcohol was affecting my suave-ability. I tried to smoulder and look sexy at Harper, but she sucked her lips into her mouth and tried not to laugh.

"He's good. He's leaving tonight. Soon, actually."

"Oh, okay. Was hoping to get to know him. Maybe next time."

"Yeah, maybe." She paused, sadness reflected in her eyes. "If there is a next time."

Dammit, Jeremy. He better not have hurt her again and told her he didn't want to see her anymore.

"I gotta go," Harper said quietly, sparing one more glance at me before turning and rushing away.

My gaze followed her all the way to bathroom.

I pushed out of the booth and stood, stretching my arms over my head as I did.

"What are you doing?"

"Toilet."

Brody looked at me, his eyebrows furrowed and

his lips pinched between his fingers.

"Seal. Broke. A lot of water. Remember?"

"Whatever."

The sadness in Harper's eyes seemed to have sobered me up somehow. I strode across the diner with long, purposeful strides, down the hall, and walked directly into the female toilets.

Chapter Twenty

Harper

Jeremy and I had spent the last few days together, catching up and getting to know one another again. He wasn't the same brother I remembered growing up. He was hard. Stronger. Angrier. But he was still my brother, and I loved him. It made having to say goodbye tonight a lot harder.

I didn't want him to go. I felt like I had just got him back and was losing him again. But he'd got a job in a garage and started tomorrow. Six hours away. So he had to get on the road tonight to make it in time for work tomorrow.

I checked my reflection in the bathroom mirror. I didn't want to look like I'd been crying and was startled when the door swung open and Nate appeared behind me.

"You shouldn't be in here," I said, catching his eyes in the mirror.

He stood right behind me, his hands resting on

my shoulders. "Just want to check on my friend."

"I'm fine." I gave him a small smile.

Nate dropped a kiss to the top of my shoulder. "You sure? Jeremy is leaving."

"I'm aware. And I'm trying not to think about it. I don't want to say goodbye to him because I don't know when I'll see him again."

"Is that why you're working tonight instead of spending time with him?" His hands drifted down my arms and circled my waist.

I nodded.

"Go spend time with him. Like you said, you don't know when you'll see him again. You don't need to be working tonight."

I sighed. He was right. I should be spending the last few hours of Jeremy's time here with him instead of cleaning tables and making milkshakes.

"Okay." I turned in his arms and looked at his bloodshot, glassy eyes. Brushing my thumb over the dark circles under his eyes, I asked, "You okay?"

Nate leaned against me, pressing me back into the counter, one hand cupping my cheek, fingers in my hair, the other dug into my hip, pinching at the skin. "No. But I'm not important. Tonight, Jeremy is important. He's where you should be."

"What happened?" I needed to know. I couldn't spend time with Jeremy if I was worrying about Nate.

"Later." He wasn't going to give me any answers yet. He reached into his pocket and pulled out his keys. "Say goodbye to Jeremy and meet me at home." He pressed his keys into the palm of my right hand and closed my fingers around them.

My stomach fluttered at his words. Home. His home, I knew, but I still liked the sound of it.

"And Brody?"

"Sneak in quietly." He pressed his lips to mine before releasing me and walking out the door.

I waited a minute or two before I left the bathroom so it didn't look like we'd been in there together and walked straight into my brother and Nate shaking hands.

"What's going on?" I forced a smile and refused to look at the bag on the floor by Jeremy's feet.

"I have to jet," Jeremy said, releasing Nate's hand. "But I'll give you a lift."

"What?" I frowned. A lift where?

"Home," Nate answered. My mouth dropped open and my eyes widened.

"Ummm. Okay." I looked over at the counter, and both Uncle Johnny and Aunt Julie waved me off.

Nate had clearly spoken to Jeremy and my uncle. I glanced at Brody, but he wasn't paying us any attention. What had he told Jeremy, though, to get him to drop me at his house?

Jeremy said goodbye to Johnny and Julie, picked up his bag, and walked out the door with me trailing behind.

"I like him," Jeremy said when got in his truck and I directed him to Nate's place.

"Me too."

"Kind of noticed that. But no one knows?"

"No." It was going to be small talk all the way to Nate's apartment, filling the silence with mindless chatter until it was time for him to walk out of my life once more.

"Why?"

"Because his cousin is my ex-boyfriend."

"The guy you were dating a few years ago? Ha! You're kidding." He was quite amused by that. "Is he good to you, though? Or do I need to kick his ass?"

"He's great. We just don't want to rush things or hurt Brody needlessly." My voice drifted off as Jeremy pulled his truck over in front of Nate's apartment.

I looked at him, and he gave me a half smile that I guessed was meant to reassure me. "I'll be back."

"Sure." I wasn't counting on it. Didn't want to get my hopes up.

"I'll visit. Come back at Christmas. It's only a few weeks away." A glimmer of hope.

"Okay." I stamped the glimmer out. I wasn't going to let myself get excited by the prospect of seeing him again.

Jeremy reached over and wrapped his arms around me. "I really did miss you. And I'm so proud of you for becoming you. I'll see you soon."

"I missed you too." I hugged him tighter. "See ya." I pulled out of his embrace and climbed out of the truck. I couldn't look at him because if I did, I'd cry. Instead, I ran up the steps and into Nate's building.

Once inside Nate's apartment, I went straight to his room, pulled a t-shirt out of his drawer, and changed into it before sliding into his bed and waiting for him to come home. Only then did I let the tears fall.

I didn't hear Nate come home.

I didn't feel him climb into bed beside me.

I didn't feel his arm wrap around my waist and hold me close.

But he was there in the morning when I woke up, tangled with his legs, my head on his chest.

"Hi, friend," he whispered as his fingers stroked my hip.

"Hi."

"You okay?"

I nodded, not wanting to talk about it. There was nothing to say. Jeremy had gone with the promises of coming back, but I wouldn't hold him to that because who knew what could happen in the next few weeks.

"Are you?" I asked, suddenly remembering he was drunk last night for some reason.

"I am now."

"Want to tell me what happened?"

"Audrey woke up, and she wants to see me."

I pulled back and lifted myself onto my elbows, watching Nate curiously. I knew he'd had so many mixed feelings over this girl. He felt guilty he couldn't save her family, and he felt bad she was alone, but he also wanted her to have a happy life and knew his parents could give her that.

"And?"

"And I'm going to see her today. With Brody." He closed his eyes.

"That's great. You might find it's just what you need. Maybe speaking to her will give you peace of mind and release some of that guilt you've been holding onto." I leaned into him and kissed him.

"I hope you're right."

"I always am."

He captured my mouth his while his hands roamed my back. "We have a few hours to kill before I have to leave."

"Oh, yeah?" I raised an eyebrow teasingly.

"Mmm-hmmm."

"What did you have in mind?" I chewed on the corner of my lip, knowing exactly what he had in mind.

"This." He peeled his shirt off me, removed our underwear, and rolled us both off the bed and onto the floor with a thud. "Oops. That was louder than I thought."

A knock sounded at the door just as Nate settled himself between my legs. Brody said through the closed door, "You okay, man?"

"Ah, yeah, I just fell out of bed that's all," he said and kissed my collarbone.

"Okay," Brody said slowly, unsure of what to think of a grown man falling out of bed.

I bit his shoulder to stifle my laughter, and Nate pressed his lips together to silence his chuckle. Brody's footsteps retreated down the hall.

"You're going to get us in trouble," he whispered.

"You're the one who rolled us on to the floor. Why didn't you just announce to Brody I was here?"

"My intentions were good," Nate murmured against my lips.

"Good…really?"

"Very good." He pushed his hips forward, and

my eyes rolled back into my head.

CHAPTER TWENTY-ONE

Nate

Dead.

They were dead.

All of them.

I was going to strangle them with my bare hands. Squeeze the life out of them.

I hated bowling.

And what was more, I hated bowling on a date.

Oh, and I hated dating…when it wasn't Harper.

And I really, really hated double dating with Brody and the two blonde bimbos Indie so happily set us up with.

Conned, more like.

Duped.

Tricked.

Whatever you wanted to call it, she did it. Rang to tell me Linc was picking me up for some event at the Surf Club that she couldn't attend because she had a meeting. The word "meeting" should have been an instant red flag. She was a graphic designer and worked from home. She didn't attend meetings. "Dress nice," she said. So, I did.

I walked into the living room to find Brody dressed equally nice, though if I was being honest, I looked better.

"Where you going?" I asked him. We'd been at the hospital again, visiting with Audrey. I'd seen her three times now, and things were getting easier.

"I have a date."

"During the day?" I laughed. What a terrible time for a date. I hope he hadn't suggested it.

"Yeah. Where are you off to?"

"A presentation for Linc."

"You his hot date?" Brody sniggered.

"Yeah. Indie couldn't make it."

A knock sounded at the door, so Brody opened it.

Indie waltzed into the room with Linc following close behind, an amused smile plastered on his smug face.

And then, out of nowhere, two blondes walked in. Twins.

"Guys, this is Cindy." Indie pointed to blonde number one. "And this is Mindy." She smiled brightly as she pointed at blonde number two.

Cindy and Mindy. No joke.

I smiled briefly in an attempt to be polite and not make them feel uncomfortable or unwanted. Even though they were.

"Can I speak to you for a minute?" I ground out. I grabbed Indie by the arm and dragged her into the hall.

"You're welcome. Mindy is lovely. Isn't she, Linc?" Indie smiled happily.

"What the hell are you doing?"

"I told you I was going to set you up."

"And I told you no!" I raised my voice. Linc stepped in front of Indie and pushed me back. As if I'd hurt her. But I did respect him a little more for protecting her over me.

"But then Linc told me your plan to set Brody up, and I thought why not set you both up."

"Why not? I'll tell you why not. Because I am not interested."

"Well, you can't very well turn them away now. Can you? That would be cruel, Nate."

I stared at her. Opened my mouth but closed it again, unsure what to say. Linc rocked on his feet, whistling softly.

Glad he was amused.

He probably put her up to it because he knew about Harper and me.

The thought of Harper had my pulse racing and stomach flipping. After the whole "just friends" thing with her brother a few days ago, things had been tense. I got the feeling she wanted to make us official or something, but I wasn't entirely sure because she wouldn't open up to me about what she was thinking or feeling.

"Get back in there and show those girls a good time." Indie ushered me back into the room. "Who knows? One might be your soulmate."

"Doubt it," I muttered under my breath. Pretty sure my soulmate was sitting on top of a water tower.

"Ready to go?" Brody asked when I returned to the living room.

"Ready as I'll ever be." Which was not at all.

I turned to speak to Indie one last time, but she and Linc had already gone. Jerks. They deserved each other.

"Let's go."

Bowling sucked.

And bowling with Cindy and Mindy sucked even more because they were more concerned with breaking a nail than knocking over any pins.

Where the hell did Indie find these girls?

Brody seemed to be enjoying himself, though. So that was good. Maybe Cindy and Mindy would be his soulmates, and then I'd be free to take Harper out on a real date and not just sleep with her.

"I'm hungry," I announced after Mindy closed out the final frame. Those two games seemed to drag on. For. Ever.

"I could eat," Brody agreed.

Yes. Maybe we could lose the girls somewhere and go get some food.

"Oooh, yes." Cindy clapped her hands. Or was it Mindy? I really couldn't tell.

"Let's go." Brody grabbed Mindy's hand and pulled her toward the door.

Cindy stared at me expectantly. Or was she Mindy and Brody had walked off with Cindy?

Shit.

I was confusing myself.

"Let's go, hot stuff." The blonde chick whose name I really didn't know skipped over to me and linked her arm through mine, pressing her body against my side.

I tried not to cringe, but I couldn't help it. Hers was not the body I wanted rubbing against mine. I recoiled slightly and faked needing to tie my laces so I could untangle myself from her. I wasn't even wearing laces, and she didn't notice I was pretending to tie air.

Yeah.

They were dead.

All of them.

***

It didn't matter how hard I argued with Brody, he wasn't taking no for answer. I tried everything. At one point, I opened the car door and tried to throw myself out because that would have been more pleasant than what was waiting for me through those doors.

Damn Johnny for making the best goddamn burgers in the state.

Why couldn't his food taste like shit? Then no one would want to stop there. If his food tasted awful, then Brody wouldn't have insisted on taking the twins there.

I felt like this whole thing was a setup.

Someone planned it this way so Harper would catch me on a date with someone else when I couldn't give her anything more than "just friends." I was really beginning to hate that word.

"Get out of the car," Brody said.

"No, you go. I'll just head home."

209

"Seriously, dude. You're acting like a tool."

We argued back and forth for ten minutes until one of the blondes climbed into the passenger seat, leaning over the console and whispering in my ear all the things she'd like to do to me.

I was out of the car in a flash. Unfortunately, so was she, and she seemed to think since she told me she wanted to tie me to her bedposts and cover me in whipped cream that we were actually dating and physical contact was perfectly fine.

She attached herself to my side. She was like a leech. Only she wasn't sucking my blood. She was sucking out my will to live.

Just kill me now.

Her arm snaked around my waist, and her hand slid into my back pocket. I moved away from her. She followed. I couldn't shake her. She was determined, I'd give her that much. But the thought of walking into the roadhouse with Airhead Barbie fused to my side made me sick. I wanted to throw up.

Reluctantly, I followed Brody and Airhead Barbie number…whatever into the diner. Maybe I'd luck out and Harper wouldn't be there. Ha. Even then, I'd still have to see the disappointment on Johnny's and Julie's faces when I walked in with someone other than their niece.

Dropping my head so I wouldn't have to see the look in anyone's eyes, I tried to remove myself from my not-date, but it only made her purr in my ear and tell me how she liked guys who played hard to get.

I wasn't playing.

I could sense her eyes on me. Cold. Hard. Hurt. I looked up and straight into the murky brown eyes of the woman I loved. No longer were they the bright sparkling caramel colour I got lost in. No. They were dead. And so was I with one glare.

She tore off her apron and slammed it on the counter, still levelling me with her glare. She had too much pride to look away or cry. I took a step forward, but the leech pulled me back.

With a slight shake of the head, I tried to convey to Harper it wasn't what it looked like. But she just curled her lip in disgust and took off into the bathroom, leaving me staring at Johnny, who was casually throwing the meat cleaver in the air and letting it stab into the bench.

Shit.

Shit.

Shit.

I'd ruined everything before it began.

They were dead.

All of them.

Slow and painful, just the way I felt right then.

CHAPTER TWENTY-TWO

Harper

I refused to cry.

I couldn't breathe. My chest constricted, and my head spun. Everything I believed, everything I thought I knew was wrong. I'd never felt my heart break before. Not like that. Not when my boyfriend in high school broke up with me. Not when Brody broke up with me. I wasn't sure I even had a heart left to break after what my parents did to me. After Jeremy left me.

But I did.

That beautiful, handsome, kind man out there pieced my heart back together and held it in his hands. I thought he'd take care of it. Cherish it.

But Nate Kellerman wasn't the guy I thought he was.

He was a liar.

A cheat.

I looked at myself in the mirror. My eyes had dimmed, glazed over with tears. I turned the tap on and splashed my face with cold water, hoping to shock my system into recovery.

He wasn't a cheat.

I couldn't honestly call him that.

We weren't in a relationship. We never were. We were just friends. He'd said it himself numerous times. I'd even tried to convince myself of it as well, but my fragile heart had other ideas, and look where that got me.

Slumped against the bathroom wall, trying not to cry over a guy who was "just a friend."

I never would have expected him to do something so hurtful. If he wanted to date other women, he should have told me, not brought one into my home, parading her around like goddamn Miss Universe. He wouldn't have to sneak her in and out of his house. Or kiss her in the shadows. He didn't have to hide her behind the bed or lie about what he was doing when he was with her.

I could hear raised voices outside the bathroom door.

Uncle Johnny threatening to slice Nate open.

Nate arguing, pleading to get past. Past where? The door, in here? I scurried into a toilet stall and locked the door.

Brody wondering what the hell was going on. Why everyone was so worked up, and why I had run off like that.

"Harper," Nate called.

"Leave. I mean it, kid," Uncle Johnny seethed, most likely holding the meat cleaver at Nate's throat…or crotch, deciding which to slice first.

"Not without speaking to her first," Nate said before shouting through the closed door, "Harper! Talk to me. It's not what you think."

"What's not what she thinks? What am I missing?"

Oh, god. Brody was going to find out.

"Johnny, please," Nate begged.

Don't let him in.

Don't let him in.

I didn't want to see him. I didn't want his pathetic excuses. I didn't want to see the sad look in his eyes. Or his beautiful smile. Because that would be my undoing. One hopeful smile from him, and I would melt in a pool at his feet. And I couldn't let that happen. I had to protect what was left of my heart. The small pile of dust it had become when he shattered it completely.

The bathroom door opened. Footsteps shuffled in. Lots of footsteps. I was still locked safely in the stall. He could try all he wanted to get me to open it, but I wouldn't.

"Harper? You okay?" Brody asked quietly.

I groaned. Why couldn't he have waited outside? This thing between Nate and me was over. There was no use in Brody finding out now. It would only needlessly hurt him.

"Go away."

"Harper." Nate banged on the door. "Talk to me. Come on." He sighed. I heard a thump. It sounded like he banged his head on the door. "We're so good at talking things through. Let me explain."

Thump.

"Explain what?" Brody was getting agitated. Confused. And he wasn't getting answers.

"I don't care what you have to say."

"You should, because I care. I care, Harper," he murmured, the pain in his voice evident through the door.

My resolved weakened, and I approached the door.

"It's not real…" *Thump*. "The date, I mean."

I braced my hands on the door, leaning forward until my head touched the cool timber, much like how I imagined Nate would be standing on the other side. How could a date not be real?

"Indie. She tried to play matchmaker."

Yeah, that sounded like Indie.

"She set us up. I thought…It doesn't matter what I thought. Point is, I didn't know. Not until it was too late."

I paused. The bathroom was silent. He was set up. And he wasn't the type of person to intentionally hurt someone's feelings. He was conned into a double date and did the right thing by Miss Universe and didn't embarrass her.

But he embarrassed me. Made me feel like a complete fool.

"Can I tell you a story?"

Yes. I stayed silent.

Feet shuffled on the other side. Someone cleared their throat.

"I don't—" Brody said, cut off by Johnny telling him to be quiet.

"I had a friend." Nate's voice was low and rough. "We were great friends. Kind of became close one night by accident, you know?"

I knew. I closed my eyes and listened to his rough voice.

"Anyway, I wasn't sure I'd ever see my friend again after…that. But I did. For three months, I had a friend I couldn't wait to see. Couldn't wait to talk to. For three months, all I could think about was my friend. It was stupid and reckless, but I didn't care. I loved spending time with them. We shouldn't have been friends, but for whatever reason, we continued our friendship in secret."

"I'm so confused," Brody mumbled.

"But after a while, my friend didn't want to be friends anymore. My friend told me we couldn't…" he paused, thinking to of the right word, I guessed, "*play* together anymore. It wasn't right. My friend was worried about getting in trouble and making our other friends jealous that we played together so much. So, I let my friend go. I promised myself that if not playing with me made my friend happy, then I'd be happy too. Harper?"

"I'm listening." I could barely get the words out from the lump in my throat.

"But I wasn't happy. I missed my friend. I missed playing together. I missed sneaking around. I just missed them. I was heartbroken. I never told my friend how I felt then, but I should have. I should have told my friend when we started playing in secret again three months later that they were the best thing that happened to me. They were my best friend."

A tear rolled down my cheek. I wiped it away. He was my best friend too.

"Do you know why, Harper?"

My heart stuttered in my chest. Taking a deep breath, I asked, "Why?"

"Because if had told my friend before how much I cared for them, I wouldn't be standing outside this door begging you to be my friend again. I wouldn't be on my knees. I wouldn't be asking you to play with me again and not keep it a secret. Screw the consequences. Will you be my friend, Harper?"

I had no resolve left. None. He broke me. Shattered. Completely.

Screw the consequences.

With trembling hands, I unlocked the door and stepped out. Nate scrambled to his feet—he really was on his knees begging—and a look of relief washed over his features.

I didn't pay attention to anyone. The only person I could concentrate on was Nate. The way he pulled me into his arms. The way he wiped the tears from my eyes. Brushed his fingers through my hair. Cupped my face and said with a smile, "I am so in love with you, friend."

My heart stopped, my knees gave out, but Nate's strong arms held me as I processed all the things he'd said. All the things I hadn't realised I was so desperate to hear.

"I'm in love with you too," I whispered against his lips.

And then…the bathroom door slammed.

We both turned to look at the vacant space Brody had just occupied.

"Touching, really. All that friend talk. But I think you might have just pissed off another one,"

Johnny said.

"Screw the consequences, right?" Nate asked, threading his fingers through mine.

"Screw everything." I nodded.

He was totally worth the risk and the fall.

Nate kissed me quickly and chased after Brody.

"This really what you want?" Uncle Johnny asked.

"It is." I smiled, even though Brody was out there hurting. I couldn't help it; I was happy. Nate loved me.

"Okay, then." Johnny wrapped an arm around my neck and kissed the top of my head. "You better get out there and make sure they don't kill each other." He chuckled as we left the bathroom.

"Come on. It won't be that bad," I scoffed. I knew Brody would be upset and angry, but he'd get over it. Right?

"You sure about that?" Johnny lifted the meat cleaver and pointed it in the direction of the parking lot.

"Shit."

Brody and Nate were rolling around on the gravel, attracting the stares of the two guys filling up their cars with fuel.

"Come on," Brody screamed and punched Nate in the face. "Fight back."

But Nate didn't. "I'm not fighting you."

They scuffled. They swore. Brody threw a few more punches, and Nate let him. After a while, Brody stopped. He must have realised Nate was letting him beat the crap out of him because Brody was hurting. An eye for an eye.

218

Brody walked away to his car and kicked the tire. Getting in the car, he slammed the door and peeled out of the parking lot, leaving nothing but a cloud of dust and his bleeding cousin behind. I wanted to follow him, chase him and explain, but I knew better. He needed time.

"Up you get." I held out my hands to help Nate up, but he pulled me down on top of him instead.

I laughed as he flipped me onto my back and ignored the pain of the gravel and stones digging into my skin. "What are you doing?"

"This." He leaned in and kissed me. It was slow. Deep. Passionate.

I sighed in contentment and brushed his hair out of his face. His lip was bleeding. There was a cut above his eye, but other than that, he looked unharmed.

"We should get you cleaned up. You're bloody and covered in dust."

"I don't think I can go home just yet." Nate kissed my neck.

"True. Come upstairs with me."

Once upstairs, I pushed him toward the bathroom and said, "Strip."

His eyes flared, a fire burning behind them as he slowly, so slowly, began removing his clothes. He raised an eyebrow. "Now what?" His voice was thick and husky and so sexy. My insides liquified.

I turned the shower on and waved him in. He shook his head and stepped toward me. "Your turn," he whispered in my ear.

I'd never really stripped for anyone before. Obviously, I took my clothes off, but it was usually rushed, frenzied as we pawed at each other, trying to get closer. I'd never actually stripped for Nate while he stood back and stared admiringly.

It was thrilling. Powerful. And so embarrassing. I was not sexy. At all. I fumbled with my shirt. Struggled to get my jeans unzipped. Almost tripped trying to pull them off. But Nate didn't seem to notice. He watched with rapt attention, taking in every detail, every curve, every flaw on my body.

"I am luckiest fucking guy in the world to get to keep you," he said and promptly picked me up, wrapping my legs around his waist before he kissed me.

"You want to keep me?" I asked as he stepped us both under the spray of the shower and backed me into the wall.

"Right here." His lips pressed into the crook of my neck. My now favourite spot for him to kiss. It never failed to send waves of delight through my body.

"Naked in the shower?" I asked, wrapping my arms around his neck as he moved my hips to align with his.

"In my arms. Forever." He wanted me forever. My heart clenched, my body ached for him, and I couldn't stop the cheesy smile from spreading across my face.

Forever.

"I'm okay with that."

Our foreheads pressed together, he pushed his hips forward, sliding into me, drowning out my moan with one of his own. "Naked in the shower works too," he breathed, bringing his mouth to mine.

Naked in the shower definitely worked.

We were so good at being friends. We played together really well. Perfectly. Amazingly.

Our tongues danced in sync with the increasing rhythm of our hips. Our hearts beat as one. Fast. Erratic. Hard. Until we pushed each other over the edge. Laboured breaths. Sloppy kisses. Heavy limbs. Happy. Content.

I was completely at his mercy, and I was okay with that.

"So, what now?" I asked after we'd finished our shower, wrapping a towel around my body. It took longer than it should because, you know, kissing. And Nate wanted to wash my hair. Which led to him washing my body. Which led to him getting distracted by my nakedness. Which in turn caused me to reciprocate.

Yeah, the shower lasted forever.

"Now, I take you on a date, friend."

"A date?" I looked up at him with wide eyes and bit my lip excitedly.

He nodded and wrapped his arms around my waist.

"Our first date?" I traced my fingers over his hard chest. The excitement was building rapidly. We'd not had a single date. How messed up was that?

He nodded again, his eyes sparkling. "In public."

I squealed just a little, and he laughed, bringing his lips to mine.

Screw the consequences.

EPILOGUE

Nate

Turned out I really didn't need therapy. I just needed Harper. I hadn't had a nightmare for weeks. Her sleeping beside me every night was enough to quiet the sounds in my head. She brought peace and calm. We weren't living together because we weren't ready for that, but if she wasn't at my place, I was staying at the roadhouse.

Brody moved out and into my parents' house while he looked for his own place. It was either that or The Love Shack, and I couldn't blame him for not wanting to stay there. I also didn't blame him for leaving. It was understandable, given the circumstances. He couldn't live in the same apartment where his ex-girlfriend spent most of her time when she wasn't at the roadhouse. I felt guilty for the way things happened, and I knew it was hard for him to see us together, but I also knew in time he'd move on and get over it.

We weren't as close as we once were. Things

were tense, and quite often he'd avoid any social situations if Harper and I were there. He still hung out with Linc and Ryder and threw himself into work. When he wasn't working, he spent all his time at the hospital with Audrey, and I visited her when he wasn't there.

My parents went and visited her frequently, spending time with her, getting to know her, and allowing her to get comfortable with them. It was awkward at first, and she didn't understand why they were coming to see her so often, but I could tell from the tiny sparkle in her eyes that she enjoyed the company.

After Christmas, we all went in together, and my parents told her they'd like for her to come and live with them, and let them give her the family and support she needed. It was an emotional day. Tears everywhere. Sad tears. Happy tears. And while Audrey was hesitant and unsure, Brody reassured her that no matter what, her family could never be replaced. She was just getting a second family who would love her as much as her own. He promised her she wouldn't be alone.

"Will you relax?" I grabbed Mum by the shoulders and forced her into an arm chair.

"What if she doesn't like the room? What if she hates the house? What if she hates us?" She sucked in a panicked breath and stood again.

"It will be okay. Just give her time."

Audrey was moving in today. Brody had gone with my dad to pick her up from the hospital, while Indie and I stayed home to help Mum prepare for her arrival.

223

"Drink this. It'll calm your nerves." Indie handed Mum a glass of wine.

"Indiana. It is ten in the morning. I am not day drinking," she said with a stern voice, nonetheless accepting the wine and gulping half of it down.

Indie smirked. "Better."

"I'm just so worried. It is going to be a big adjustment for all of us."

"We'll get through it together. Don't worry." I squeezed her shoulder gently and sat on the coffee table in front of her.

Audrey had a long way to go to recover fully, and I wasn't sure she would ever completely get over what happened. She was going to need more skin grafts, more surgeries, and a hell of a lot of therapy to help her deal with her emotions, but if anyone could work through it with her and be there for her, it was our parents.

The front door opened, and Dad walked in first. Mum launched out of the chair and stood on the threshold of the living room, tears in her eyes as Brody escorted Audrey up the front porch and into the foyer. It was a slow process. She was still in pain, her movements slow and jerky from the tightness of her skin grafts. Her head was down, and she had her arm hooked through Brody's.

"Hi, Audrey," Mum said with a soft smile, discreetly wiping a tear as it slid down her cheek. "Welcome home."

Audrey didn't speak. She simply nodded once.

Mum frowned in disappointment but quickly pushed the feeling aside.

"Let's show you to your room. Shall we?"

No reaction. Just a small step closer to Brody.

"Come on," he said quietly. "It's okay."

The poor girl. I was surprised she was doing so well, to be honest. No way could I have moved in with a family I didn't know. The bitterness and resentment I would feel at losing my own would send me spiralling out of control.

Brody led her down the hall and into my father's study. We'd decided it would be easier for Audrey if she didn't have to walk up and down the stairs all the time to get to her room.

"I wasn't sure what sort of things you liked, or what your favourite colour is, so I kept it white and grey and added a few feminine touches, a little bit of pink and mint. I hope that's okay?" my mother prattled on nervously.

Indie rolled her eyes.

I was positive the last thing Audrey cared about was the décor in her new room.

"We also filled the closet with clothes for you. I wasn't sure what your style was," she said, opening the closet. Again, I doubted Audrey cared about clothes in that moment, but I knew my mother meant well. "The doctors suggested to keep things light and loose so it didn't...it didn't hurt your...well, anyway, if you don't like them or you don't like your room, we can always change it to suit you. That's not a problem." Mum took a deep breath and clasped her hands together in front.

Audrey was still staring at her feet. Still huddled against Brody. "What do you think?" he asked.

A nod. That was it. I guessed it was better than no response at all.

225

"Come on, love, let's leave Audrey to get settled in." My dad wrapped his arm around Mum and pulled her from the room.

"But what if she's hungry? I didn't ask. Oh, my goodness, what a terrible host I am." Mum gasped and turned back around. "Would you like something to eat, Audrey? It was a long drive."

Audrey shook her head.

"Okay, tell me if you change your mind. This is your home now, and we want you to feel as comfortable as possible. We're so happy to have you here, sweetheart." Mum rushed out of the room, wiping at her eyes again.

Indie and I stood awkwardly in Audrey's room. Neither of us knew what to say as Brody helped her out of her jacket.

"It really is nice to have you here, Audrey." Indie smiled. "I'm sure we're going to be great friends. Come on, Nate." She grabbed my hand and dragged me out of the room when Audrey didn't respond.

"That went well," she said when we walked into the kitchen where Dad was making coffee.

"I think so. It'll take a while for her to settle in and get used to everyone," I agreed.

"Oh, shoot. We have to go," Indie said as she glanced at the clock on the wall.

"Call if you need anything." Indie and I took turns giving Mum a kiss on the head. She didn't even notice. She was staring absently out the patio doors.

"We'll be fine," Dad said, clapping me on the back and kissing Indie's cheek. "Go. Say goodbye to Jack for us."

Jack was heading back to uni, and we were meeting at the diner so he could have one last burger before he left, since Ryder flat-out refused to cook for him.

Word had somehow gotten out that Johnny had the best burgers in town, and business picked up. So much so that he had to hire staff and permanently left a reserved sign on our booth. When we walked in, the place was bustling with people. The jukebox was cranking out fifties tunes. The scent of burgers and fried onions wafted through the air.

Warm hands wrapped around my waist from behind. "How did it go?" Harper asked into my back. I turned in her arms and angled her face up to mine.

"And I'll be leaving now," Indie said, screwing her face up in disgust as I leaned down and pressed my lips to Harper's.

"Good as could be expected. It'll take a while, though."

"Sorry I wasn't there. Didn't want to make it any more awkward."

"You're here now." I brushed her hair out of her face. "And I think Brody living there will help immensely."

"Why do you say that?"

"Guess all that time he spent with her in the hospital bonded them or something. She trusts him."

"That's good. He cares. That's what makes him good at his job."

We walked over to the booth and sat down.

A young girl, no more than fifteen, came to take

our order, but Harper told her not to worry about it. Johnny knew we were there, and he also knew what to cook.

Burgers.

"Where's Kenzie?" Indie frowned and slid into the booth next to Linc.

"Umm…" Bailey glanced at Ryder nervously. His hands were clenched, and he was rapping his knuckles on the table. "Dealing with Chace."

"What happened?" Harper pulled out a chair.

"He showed up at the apartment last night, drunk as anything, demanding to see Cole."

Everyone looked at Ryder as he ground his teeth. "I didn't do anything," he said in answer to our unspoken question.

"I find that hard to believe." Linc laughed.

"No, really. Kenzie called the police and didn't tell us until this morning."

"Really?"

"She's worried about Ryder. Doesn't want him getting in any more trouble." Bailey rubbed her fingers over Ryder's knuckles, and he relaxed.

"Ha. Trouble finds Ryder wherever he goes. He's like a magnet," Jack said as the doors to the diner opened and closed once more.

"What the hell are you doing here?" Johnny's voice called from the kitchen as he threw what sounded like a pan into the sink at the same time Jack whistled.

"Lookin' for a place to stay. You got one?" someone answered in a vaguely familiar but rough voice that sounded like they'd smoked too many cigarettes.

"Depends." Johnny chuckled.

Resting his head in his hands, his eyes bugging out of his head, Jack asked, "Who is that?"

We all turned to see who had caused such a commotion in the kitchen and that much admiration from Jack.

Johnny came out of the kitchen as the guy dropped his bags at his feet, brushed a hand through his hair.

"You stayin' permanently?" Johnny asked and pulled him in for a hug.

"I hope so."

"Then I got a place to stay." Johnny smiled and pointed his spatula directly at Harper.

The guy turned around, and Harper burst into tears.

"Jeremy."

Sneak Peek

KENZIE AND THE GUY NEXT DOOR

Novel #4

R. LINDA

CHAPTER ONE

Kenzie

The thumping of the bass was killing me. A slow, tortured, sleep-deprived death. I buried my head under the pillow for the third night in a row. Now, I wasn't against music. Quite the opposite, actually. I had amassed a pretty decent collection of classic rock albums on vinyl. But what I did oppose was the amp being switched to eleven all night long while my child and I tried to sleep.

My bedroom door opened, and Cole stumbled in, rubbing the sleep out of his eye with his teddy wedged tightly under his arm. "Mumma, I can't sleep."

Dammit.

"Come here, honey." I opened my arms for him, and he climbed in bed beside me.

"They're very noisy, aren't they?"

"They are. I'll go and speak to them tomorrow and tell them to keep it quiet from now on."

"Can you tell them now, so I can sleep?" He

yawned and snuggled into my pillows.

I banged my fist against the wall and listened for the music to soften. It didn't. In fact, I was pretty sure they cranked it even higher.

"You stay right here. I'll be back in a minute." I kissed his blond curls and climbed out of bed, cursing my new neighbour I hadn't even met yet, let alone seen, as I went in search for my keys.

I was only going to knock on the door and politely demand they shut their music off at a decent hour so I wouldn't have to resort to shoving my foot up their ass. I'd be gone for two minutes, max. But no way was I leaving my apartment unlocked. Chace had been hanging around for weeks. Constant phone calls. Text messages. Showing up outside. Demanding to see his son. Over my dead body.

So, I locked the door as a precaution. I didn't trust Chace. At all. Each time I saw him, he appeared more and more deranged. He'd disappear for a week or two, only to show up again an absolute wreck. I didn't know what I saw in him when I was fourteen. He was a complete narcissist. If I had more money, I'd pack Cole up and move us into a nice house with a back yard, where Chace couldn't find us, but I didn't. So, we lived in a shoebox of an apartment, with noisy neighbours and disappearing keys.

Where the hell were they? I checked the fruit bowl, the hook by the door, my handbag, the TV unit, the coffee table, kitchen table, the freezer, the microwave, inside my leather boots—all the usual places, but they were nowhere to be seen. I cursed to myself and began flipping the cushions on the sofa, pulling Cole's toys out of the basket in the living room. And then I searched the kitchen and the pantry.

Ah-ha! In the cookie jar. Of course. Cole had been playing with the keys, driving the cookies around the table like cars, after dinner.

I grabbed them out and walked to the door, making sure to lock it behind me. Casting a nervous glance down the hall to make sure no one was lurking, I padded over to the next apartment. It was bad that I worried about someone hiding in the shadows, but I wouldn't put it past Chace to do just that.

The music was so loud I doubted they'd hear me knock. Regardless, I bashed both my fists against the door for added affect. I didn't expect the door to swing open, though. And I certainly didn't expect to come face to face with a naked chest.

I dropped my eyes to floor, taking in my neighbour's bare feet, black track suit pants, letting my gaze wander of the expanse of his chest, the tattoos that beautifully decorated his pecs, arms, shoulders, and finally looked at his face.

Him.

I knew him. I just didn't know how I couldn't have known he was my new neighbour. Surely, it would have come up in conversation at some point over the last couple of weeks.

He grinned and flicked a black lock of hair out of his face before holding up one finger, indicating I should wait.

Why should I wait for him?

I was there for a reason.

He turned and walked into his living room, over to his stereo, and lowered the volume. Meanwhile, I stared at the muscles in his back, the way they moved and tensed as he leaned down and picked up a shirt.

"Can I help you with something?" He smirked, sliding his grey t-shirt over his head and restricting my view of his abs.

My mouth watered.

Oh, my god. What was wrong with me?

"Turn your goddamn music down. I have a child who is trying to sleep next door," I growled at him.

He looked at me, then at the stereo, cupping his hand around his ear. "Hear that?" he asked. "No music."

"Let's keep it that way. Yeah?"

He shrugged. "You live next door?"

"Clearly." I turned and stormed out.

"Wait," he called after me.

I stopped and turned to face him, crossing my arms over my chest. "What?"

His eyes darkened as he looked my body up and down, not once, but twice. Wiping his mouth, he said, "I'm sorry about the noise, babe."

I scoffed. "The sincerity of that apology was shot to hell the moment you called me babe. I'm not your babe." I stalked out of his apartment.

"But you are one," he said, sticking his head out the door.

"One what?" I paused with my key in the lock. I was asking for trouble simply by standing near him.

"A babe."

"Yeah, I get that all the time." I laughed humourlessly. "You're a pig."

"What? You got a great ass."

"You did not just say that." I acted offended, when in reality, it was kind of nice to hear. No one had ever told me I had a great ass before. No one had ever called me a babe.

"Not my fault you stormed into my living room looking sexy as hell in that." He gestured to my clothes, and I cursed myself for forgetting to put something on over my tank top and short shorts.

"Just keep the music down, okay?" I said, trying to keep my voice even and not let on that he affected me with his words.

"Sure thing, babe." I opened the door to my apartment and was closing it when he called out again. "And, Kenzie?" I closed my eyes and willed him to shut up. "I think we're going to be great neighbours."

I shut the door without a word, hearing him chuckle softly from the other side.

Cole was fast asleep when I returned the bedroom, curled on his side with the bear Bailey had bought him when she and Ryder left for uni nestled under his chin.

I tiptoed back out to the kitchen for a glass of water. My throat was dry, and a light sheen of sweat coated my skin. It wasn't an overly warm night, but my body was buzzing, flooded with warmth. I refilled my glass and took it back to bed with me, deciding to settle on top of the covers, hoping I'd cool down.

I closed my eyes and waited for sleep to overtake

me. I was exhausted after not getting enough rest the past few nights, no thanks to my cocky neighbour. Sleep didn't come, though. Instead, I was plagued by images of tattooed torsos and loose pants hanging dangerously low on very defined hips. I was haunted by whiskey coloured eyes and that rough voice repeating the word 'babe' over and over.

I tossed and turned and eventually settled for watching a movie in the living room since I had no doubt I'd fail to sleep again tonight, and it had nothing to do with loud music.

It had everything to do with the way my new neighbour made me feel.

Damn Jeremy Donovan—Harper's brother.

Acknowledgements

As always, I'd like to thank my children and partner for their support and for understanding when I spend many sleepless nights and long days locked away in my office to finish a book. I love you.

My family and friends for the continued support and encouragement and for actively taking an interest in my dreams. I appreciate you.

Limitless Publishing for sticking with me, for all your assistance in the publishing process. You took a chance on an unknown author, and I am forever grateful. You are an amazing team to work with.

I also must thank my amazing editor Lori, once again, for dealing with my penchant for run on and fragmented sentences and my complete lack of organisation. Maybe by the end of the series, I'll be less of a mess. You are amazing.

Huge thanks to Deranged Doctor Designs for this epic cover design. It's absolutely stunning. You are incredible.

Also, a huge thank you to Amber because really, she's the bee's knees. Without your assistance along the way, I would have drowned under piles of to-do lists. You're my lifesaver.

And lastly, it goes without saying, but I need to thank my research assistant, the Sam to my Dean, my BBF Fiona Keane. Again, you kept me sane, always there with much needed advice and ideas, brainstorming with me or just sending me unnecessary but much appreciated GIFs and messages to help the creative process. I adore you.

About the Author

R. Linda drinks wine and writes books.

A coffee-addicted, tattoo-enthusiastic fangirl with a slight obsession for a particular British boy band and solo artist, she is a writer of Contemporary YA/NA Romance and Suspense, sometimes dabbling in Paranormal as well.

Renee lives in Melbourne, Australia, with her husband and two sons. When not writing, she can often be found reading books to her children and cuddling up with them on the couch to watch their favourite movies.

Connect with R. Linda:

Facebook:
https://www.facebook.com/rlindanovels/

Instagram:
https://www.instagram.com/rlindaauthor

Twitter:
https://www.twitter.com/rlindawrites

Website:
https://www.rlindanovels.com

Pinterest:
https://www.pinterest.com/abookishdelight

Get up close and personal with R. Linda along with some sneak peeks and exclusive giveaways and more in her reader group.

Reader Group:
https://www.facebook.com/groups/3404941863672 86/

Never miss an update. Get a free short story when you subscribe to my newsletter.
https://www.rlindanovels.com/subscribe

Be sure to sign up for my monthly newsletter to stay up to date on all upcoming releases, sales, giveaways, and more.
https://www.rlindanovels.com/subscribe